Trixie Tempest

and the Witches' Academy

by Ros Asquith

HarperCollins *Children's Books*

For Jessie

First published in Great Britain by HarperCollins **Children's Books** in 2004
HarperCollins **Children's Books** is a division of HarperCollins **Publishers** Ltd
77-85 Fulham Palace Road, Hammersmith, London W6 8JB

www.harpercollinschildrensbooks.co.uk

1 3 5 7 9 8 6 4 2

Text and illustrations copyright © Ros Asquith 2004
ISBN 0 00 714424 5

Ros Asquith asserts the moral right to be
identified as the author and illustrator of the work.

Printed and bound in England
by Clays Ltd, St Ives plc

Chapter 1

It's happened! Every ten-year-old in the country has one big dream and it's the SAME dream. And it's happened to me! I have a real proper letter inviting me to go to Hogwarts School of Witchcraft and Wizardry. Oh no, you think this is a joke, don't you? Someone, probably my tricky friend Dinah Dare-deVille, is pulling the old wool over the eyes of me, Trixie Tempest. But no. This is for real. Well, wait, it isn't Hogwarts exactly, but it will be just the same, I know it.

It happened first post this very morning, when an owl just swooped into the kitchen... (oh all right, I made that bit up);

when the postman stumped up the path and was leapt on, as usual, by my dog Harpo and a bundle of puppies. I think they like his dreads. Luckily, he is a kindly postman who likes dogs.

"Recorded delivery!" he bellowed, causing everyone to rush headlong into the hall except me. Well, it's not my birthday and I don't have a pen friend, though I would like one. So I took the chance to get a whole bowlful of Krispy Popsickles. Hah!

Why was my small cannonball of a brother, Tomato, hurtling to the door, do you think? It's because he has sent off fifty-two Krispy Popsickle tokens that he has been collecting since he was three, to get a light sabre.

Why was my father hurtling to the door? (This is a bit sad really; he has been collecting tokens too, for a half-price workbench that my mother says he already has three of and what use could he possibly find for another.)

Why was my mother hurtling to the door? Because she has taken the day off work to wait in for some boring furniture. Why does she think the postman is delivering furniture? Why do I care, I'm on my second bowl of Krispy Popsickles.

"It's for you, Trix," says Mum.

"S'mine s'mine s'my light sabre s'mine!" bellows Tomato. "It says T Tempest, so tis mine."

He is getting very good at letters for a four-year-old, but Mum has to restrain him from ripping open the long purple (yes!) envelope with the curly

gold (double yes!) writing on
and the owl (really) stamp,
Highlands and
Islands.

Miss T. Tempest

"Tomato," I said kindly,
"it says *Miss* T. Tempest. And you are not
a *Miss*, are you?"

"Oh my godfathers," squeaked Dad, sitting
down rather suddenlyish. "I wonder if that's what
I think it is."

Everyone gave him a funny look. He was a very
pale shade of pale. I didn't know what he was
talking about, of course, until I opened it. And
there it was, every ten-year-old's dream come
true. If you don't believe me, here's the letter:

CONUNDRUMS ACADEMY

Dear Trixie Tempest,

A place has been secured for you on Conundrums Academy's half-term taster course in Witchcraft and Wizardry. Although it is a most unusual step for us to accept English children of no obvious talent, we have done so at the request of your grandmother, the High Priestess of Egg, Eugenia Tempest, who was herself a pupil here and has generously agreed to pay the fees for this week-long course.

If you show promise, you may be accepted as a full-time pupil at Conundrums.

Please indicate your acceptance of our terms on the accompanying form.

Yours faithfully,

Marcia Wince

Academy Secretary

Well, apart from that bit about no obvious talent (they should hear me play my trumpet, they should see me play football), that has to be the most exciting thing that has ever happened, as I'm sure you'll agree. Though, of course, being descended from seventeen generations of witches ought to give me a natural advantage, and explains why Grandma Tempest is paying the fees.

First thing I did next after opening this was let out a WHOOP the size of an elephant and leap on the table, scattering rather a lot of puppies. (Yes, I'm afraid Harpo has no control over them and they just do what they like, now they have discovered that if you jump on to the vegetable trolley and from there on to the chair, it's only a little scramble on to the table and then only a second or two to the nearest bowl of Krispy Popsickles.)

"Calm down, you're late for school already," snapped mum, looking at Dad with something very like furious fury. He gave her an "it's not my fault" shrug. "Something to do with Grandma Tempest, I suppose," said Mum. "Can I see it?"

"'Course you can," I said innocently, unaware of the stormy storm that was brewing. "It's the best thing that ever happened to me, the best best best." And I flung her the letter and jumped down to do a war dance with Tomato, Harpo and all five puppies.

"It's 8.30, get your skates on," was all my mum said, but what did I care?

"Gotta get a pen, gotta get a pen, gotta get a stamp," was all I could say as I hurtled to the hall and rootled furiously around in my school bag for a working biro. Well, you know what that's like; all I found were three dried-up felt-tips and a chewed pencil.

"Who's got a PEN?" I shouted.

"You don't need one now, your pencil is fine for school. Get going," snarled Mum, thrusting my packed lunch at me. Goodness, she must have got out of bed the wrong side. Why was she so upset that it wasn't her silly old furniture stuff?

"But I've got to sign the acceptance form and send it off!" I squeaked.

"You mean WE have to," said my mum, waving the form at me as though it was a letter from jail. Oh. Well, yes, it did say signature of parent or guardian.

"Oh, never mind," I trilled, a rather sinky sort of feeling coming over me. "I can forge that."

Mum gave me one of her Very Extremely teachery looks.

"You will do it? Please? *Pretty please?*" I begged. Sometimes I wish I had a tail to wag so I could be as sweet as the puppies.

"We'll talk about it after school," she said, with a kinder face.

It was that kinder face that was getting to me all the way to school. It was a kind of breaking-the-news-gently face. Mum didn't want me to go to Conundrums. I knew it in my boots. I would have to rely on Dad.

I hurtled into school just in time for registration. It's quite good having a T name, because if you're late, you still squash in and don't have to go in the late book. My best-friends-in-the-world, Dinah (Dare-deVille) and Chloe (Caution), are not so lucky. Chloe would never be late as she is Miss Goodums and if anyone shouts at her she turns into a little pink puddle, so even the dreaded Warty-Beak, our horrendous supply teacher, can hardly bring himself to be mean to her. Mind you, Warty-Beak's kindest mood is like other people's most disgustrous one.

Chloe was blushing in the corner. Someone must have said "hello" to her – that always makes her blush – and wouldn't catch my eye. I was desperate to tell her and Dinah about Conundrums – and Dinah wasn't there!

Of course, Dinah sneaked in even later than me and did not escape the infrared peepers of the Warty-Beak, who immediately put her down in the late book and made her take the register to Old Hedake, the head teacher. Curses! You only get two chances to talk before lunch time. One is after registration and the other is at break. I had to sit through Numeracy (that thing we used to call Maths) and Literacy (used to be reading, I think)

under the numbing gaze of the Warty, who foiled all my attempts to signal to my chums. I finally managed to scribble a note:

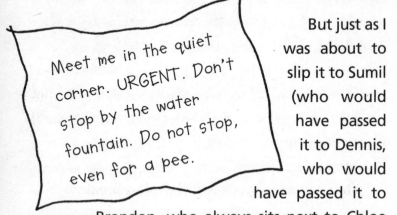

Meet me in the quiet corner. URGENT. Don't stop by the water fountain. Do not stop, even for a pee.

But just as I was about to slip it to Sumil (who would have passed it to Dennis, who would have passed it to Brandon, who always sits next to Chloe because she gives him sweeties), old Warty hovered up.

"D'you like it, Sir?" I smiled up at him with my nicest smile. "It's how I think my hero would write to his friend."

"I had thought your hero was a nineteenth-century chimney sweep, Patricia," said Warty, with some justification, since that is what I had told him I was writing about. Why does he call me Patricia? He knows I hate it. On he drones... "I hardly think that water fountains were abundant among the chimney-sweep population, though doubtless they would have been glad of such amenities. And do you think he would have used the word 'PEE'?" he added, as a ripple of giggles ran round the class.

Warty Beak in a nice mood

"Er, what would he have said?" I asked innocently.

But that was a question too far. Warty changed from his usual mottled green to a rather violent pink.

"Stay in and we'll discuss it during break."

So just when I am bursting to tell my friends about the most exciting thing that has ever happened to me (sorry if you are someone who goes to witchy school already, or are a champion sky diver or something, you probably think I am Very Extremely boring and you should be reading *Silence of the Lambs*) I am kept in for break and don't get a chance to see them till lunch time.

After a gazillion years of toiling under the beak of Warty, it was time for lunch. I grabbed Dinah and

Chloe and hauled them off to the quiet corner.

"What about my lunch?" wailed Chloe, who is one of the few Year Fives who actually likes school meals. She ENJOYS that semolina thingy with the little blob of jam in the middle.

"Chloe, share mine. This is important."

It was hard to sacrifice my Cheesy Strings. But worth it. I told them. It was better than they thought. Their jaws really did drop, like in stories.

"Oh, wait a minute," said Dinah. "It's a kid-on. Nice one, Trix."

Loony-balloony, with friends like these who needs enemies? "It's not, honest. You know I'd never make a joke about something... so... amazing," I said.

"Of course she wouldn't," said kind, trusting Chloe.

"True. You'd be scared of turning into a pumpkin or something," said Dinah, slightly less kindly. "Show us the letter, then."

"You'll have to come back after school, I had to leave it for my folks to sign. And—" I could feel a strange trembly feeling, almost like I was about to cry, which I certainly wasn't "—and I don't think they'll sign it."

"What?!" shouted Dinah. "That's outrageous."

"Oh, Trixie, do you want a tissue?" asked Chloe.
Sometimes Chloe can be a just a little bit too
sympathetic...

"Of course they'll sign it," said good old
optimistic Dinah. "If they don't, there's always
torture, heh heh."

"Maybe we could get *your* folks to persuade
them," I said. "Get your mum to tell my mum it's
the chance of a lifetime. And that she'd certainly
send you if it was *her* choice."

"I wish it *was* me," said
Dinah fiercely. "You're
soooooo lucky."

"Maybe you could both
come too," I said. "I could
get a big long cloak and
sit on Chloe's shoulders,
with the cloak wrapped
round both of us, and, er,
you could dress up
as an animal, a lion
maybe..."

"A lion?!" said Dinah.

"Yes, you know, witches always have cats or owls or something with them, don't they, so why not a lion? That way we could all get in."

"Trixie Tempest," said Chloe. "You live in dreamland."

I think Chloe might grow up to be a teacher. I'm sorry to say it, of a friend and so on, but she does have a Very Extremely teachery way with her at times.

Well, of course, a horrible thought nagged me all the rest of the day: supposing the letter was a joke? Supposing my archenemies Orange Orson or Grey Griselda had sent it to wind me up? I knew Griselda had overheard me talking about my witchy relations to Chloe and Dinah once and she'd gone on about it ever since, whenever she got the chance. Like, "Ooh, here comes Witchy Tempest. Hey, Witchy, if you're so magic, how come you can't make that ugly mug of yours disappear and put something better on top of your neck?" Or, "There obviously isn't a spell for cleverness in your family, is there, or dress sense? Or popularity?" Of course, I'd pretended it was all a joke. I mean, being related to witches isn't what you want going all round school, is it?

I didn't dare say I thought the letter *might* be a joke, to Dinah and Chloe. I was sure when I saw the Conundrums headed notepaper again, it would be all right, but of course on the way home from school, wet blanket Chloe put her oar in.

"You don't suppose *someone else* has sent the letter as a joke, do you?" she said, in her most concerned and worried voice. "I mean, it does seem rather unlikely that there really is a school for witches. Doesn't that sort of thing only happen in books?"

"Of course it's real," said Dinah crossly. But I could see she thought exactly the same thing and I was feeling on the small side, which is not hard for someone knee high to a pea in the first place.

We walked home at snail-racing speed. But when we got to mine, things got worse.

Chapter 2

"Trixie, we've got to talk," shouted my mum, bustling out of the kitchen the minute she heard me. "Oh, hello, Dinah. Hello, Chloe." Her face fell. "I'm awfully sorry sweethearts, but I can't give you tea today, there's been a little family, um, thing."

"What?" I cried.

"Oh, it's nothing awful, really, no one's ill or anything," she said, looking at my face which I think must have had the scared-stiff expression of a scared-stiff person all over it. "I'm really sorry girls, but do come over tomorrow instead, won't you?"

"Oh, that's OK," said Dinah and Chloe, backing off down the path and thinking, obviously, that the whole thing *had* been a joke.

The minute they'd gone, Mum called Dad, who came in dragging a plank (he is always dragging planks about, I think they are a bit like Tomato's blanket that he still takes to bed with him and chews all night). So Tomato has a security blanket and Dad has, well, a security planket. I was just chuckling at this thought, when Mum said sharply, "I'm afraid this isn't funny, Trix. Oh, Tobias, put that down!"

She only calls dad Tobias when she is Very Extremely upset. I rearranged my face to be serious. Now I knew no one had died, I just wanted to get on with persuading them about the Conundrums letter, as long as it was real, of course.

"Where is my Conundrums letter?" I couldn't help asking.

"Conundrums is out of the question, I'm afraid..."

"It's not a trick letter, is it?"

"What? Oh no, I don't think so." Mum looked distracted, but I breathed a sigh of relief.

"Yippeeeeeeeeeeee eeeeeeeee!" I squeaked, swinging a couple of puppies round my head and dancing a jig.

"TRIXIE! Listen!"

So I did. And then I realised the *real* reason that she and Dad had thundered to the door this morning so fast. It wasn't about waiting in for furniture and workbenches. They were waiting for a man from the bank. Apparently Dad had lost a Very Extremely big amount of money, which he had paid for a whole lot of DIY gadgets with, that he had got very cheap and was hoping to sell to make lots of money, but these thingamajigs, whatever they were, had had something wrong with them and had all had to be scrapped.

"Well, surely he could still have sold them?" I asked.

"They were dangerous, you see," said Mum. "They might have hurt someone."

I wish she wouldn't talk to me in that teachery way as if I was about five when anything serious happens. Well, it's obvious that if something's dangerous it can hurt someone, isn't it?

Meanwhile, Dad was looking at the floor (which is all made of planks, of course, so is probably a Very Extremely comforting place for him to look) and muttering that he was sure he could have fixed them and now was the time, if ever there was one, to go and get that *cup*.

A *cup*? I hope Dad is not going mad.

"Well, never mind," I said, thinking these adult money worries were a bit dull and they needed to enjoy life a bit more. "You can always get some more that aren't dangerous, can't you, Dad?"

"No, Trix," said Mum. "What I'm trying to tell

you is that we are badly in debt. We owe a lot of money. The man from the bank came this morning and we had to go through everything and we have to be very, very careful with money, otherwise in three months' time…" I saw Dad give her a sharp kick under the table "…things may get worse."

"If I had hung on to that *cup*, none of this would ever have happened," said Dad.

"Oh, shut up about that stupid *cup*," snapped Mum.

"Oh, three months is ages," I said cheerily. "I'm sure something will turn up."

But my father was babbling about teacups and my mother looked on the edge of tears, and I was getting a strong feeling that bringing up Conundrums again might not be too popular. Luckily we were saved by the door bell as Tomato was delivered back from tea with his best fiend, Bush. He came rolling in covered in ketchup and since he was in one of his cuddly moods, me, Mum, Dad, Harpo and the puppies were pretty soon covered in ketchup too. It was just the kind of light relief we needed.

"Don't tell Tomato," hissed Mum. "It'll only worry him."

We had fish fingers and beans for tea and Mum seemed quite normal, so I asked for my letter again.

"Oh, yes," she said, distractedly and fished it out from under a boring looking pile of bills and bank stuff and things with FINAL DEMAND stamped on them in red.

"What's a final demand?" I asked.

"OH, um... just a bill you have to pay now," she said.

I looked at my lovely Conundrums letter again. And at the envelope.

"This is a real letter, isn't it?" I asked.

"Oh yes, it's real all right," said Dad.

I could see Mum looking very grumpy.

"Look, Trixie," she said, "I've just explained to you why you can't possibly go. We can't expect Grandma Tempest to pay for the fares as well as a week's fees, and you'd have to have a cloak and a spell book too. It all costs money. It just can't be done. And that's final."

Cloak! Spell book! I HAVE to go.

"Mum, just because you've got money worries doesn't mean you have to make everyone else miserable too." Then I had a good idea. "Dad," I said, "why don't you come for a walk with me and Harpo?" I knew, if I could get Dad on his own, I could make him see my side.

"Great idea," he said, putting down his plank.

Harpo had heard the word "walk" and started going bonkers. Once she hears it, you have to get out of the house with her pretty quick or she starts eating the furniture. I think she is getting a bit bored of looking after the puppies all day and is longing for her freedom, a bit like Mum.

"You will let me go to Conundrums, won't you, Dad?" was the first thing I said, as soon as we turned into the park and let the raving heffalumph Harpo off the lead.

"I would if it was up to me, Trix."

"Well it's just as much up to you as it is to Mum," I said.

"No. Mum has the purse strings," he said sadly. "I've really botched it up and, well, things are worse than we let on just now?"

"Tell me. How bad are they?" I said, taking him seriously for the first time.

"Well, I don't like to worry you, but maybe it's better you know, then you won't feel so cross with Mum about Conundrums."

"Yes. Tell me."

We sat on a park bench. Harpo had found her beloved Lorenzo, the posh red setter who lives next door and has the honour of being father to our beautiful puppies, and she'd run off into the bushes with him for a doggy snog.

"OK, here goes, we've got just three months to try and get back the money I lost or they will come and repossess the house. That means we will have to leave Bottomley and go into a small flat somewhere much cheaper."

"They'll take away our HOUSE?" Whoopsy. Things were worse than I had thought.

"If only I had that *cup*," Dad said again.

"Lorenzo! Lorenzo!"

Oh godfathers, it was Mrs Next-Door, who doesn't like to let Lorenzo out of her sight for one second, rampaging towards us, her face like a sockful of chisels.

"Where is he?" she demanded.

"In the bushes with Harpo," said Dad, before I could shut him up.

"Well, reeeeeally!" screeched Mrs Next-Door. "I hope you've had her spayed, we don't want another set of mongrels, do we?"

Goodness, I thought she liked the puppies. But she doesn't like anything, except Lorenzo, of course. She stomped off and emerged from the bushes with Lorenzo in her arms.

"There, there, little Lorenzokins," she muttered.

"Ooo doesn't want to be a daddy again, does oo? Too much responsibility."

There there little Lorenzokins

Cheek! Lorenzo does nothing for those puppies. Harpo does all the work. Poor old Harpo followed glumly, and glumly we walked home. Conundrums seemed unlikely now.

I went to bed early and read my letter again. Surely I could forge a signature? Then I could hitchhike to Scotland and say I'd been robbed of my cloak and spell book and money. They wouldn't turn me away if I got all the way there, surely? I clutched my witchy amulet that Grandma Tempest had given me and wished and wished as hard as I could to go to Conundrums. Then I wished my folks would get money from somewhere. Then I wished we would not have to lose our house. But to be honest, at that time, it just didn't seem likely. It just seemed like a boring old thing adults worry about. All I could think about was getting to Conundrums.

At 6 a.m. I woke with a start. My bed was full of puppies and Tomato. Bonzo always sleeps with me, but the rest of the puppies always sleep with Tomato and sometimes if he comes into my bed at night they all follow him. I had been dreaming. In my dream, Dad was trapped in a giant teacup and shouting, "If only I had the *cup*, if only I had the *cup*."

"But you're IN the *cup*, Dad," I was telling him. "You're right inside it, can't you see?"

What was it about this *cup*? I woke up feeling sure that either Dad was going mad, or this *cup* was somehow the solution to all our problems.

I slipped out of bed, managing not to wake a single Tomato or puppy, and crept downstairs. I would make Dad a nice cup of tea and then see if I could find out more...

Unfortunately I tripped over Dad's slippers and the whole cup of tea went over him, but never mind, it was a good way of getting him up at the crack of dawn – and  Mum didn't wake! Well, she did mutter something about selling her Diamond Togetherness Ring, but she was fast asleep. Oh dear, Mum is thinking of selling her most precious ring that Dad gave her. Obviously things are bad if she's thinking about that in her sleep...

Dad stumbled down with me and I quizzed him

about the *cup*. "Dad, why do you keep going on about some old teacup?"

"What?" He looked completely baffled.

"You keep moaning on about a cup, and if only you had it now everything would be all right."

"Oh, the *CUP*," he said, a little light bulb coming on over his head.

"Yes, the *CUP*," I said, patiently.

"Oh, the *CUP*."

I felt this could go on a long time.

"Tell me about it."

"It's not a teacup. It's an incredibly beautiful, splendid, golden cup."

"A VALUABLE *cup*?" I was cheering up.

"Oh, yes. Worth a small fortune."

I had learnt that when adults say something is worth a small fortune that it is, in fact, worth a Very Extremely large fortune. I was feeling definitely cheery.

"And it's yours?"

"Oh, yes. My great-great-grandfather won it at a game of Snarg. It was the grandest wizard's trophy at Conundrums..."

"You mean your great-great-grandfather went to Conundrums?"

"Of course, and this cup was the only Conundrums trophy that was passed from father to son. Once it was in the family it stayed in the family for ever. All you had to do was to play Snarg to keep it. But if you were good at Snarg, you got your name put on the cup in diamonds... and well... I was good at Snarg and so..."

"Hang on a minute, I'm lost. What IS Snarg?"

"Conundrums' main sport, oh, it's a wonderful game." Dad looked dreamy.

"You mean *you* played Snarg?"

"Of course, everyone did."

"What do you mean, everyone?"

"Well, everyone who went to Conundrums."

"You mean *you* went to Conundrums?!!"

"Of course."

"You never told me!"

"You never asked."

Look, I have to break off here to say I was well and truly gobsmacked. I couldn't believe my lugholes. My own dad had been to Conundrums, the witches' academy, and had never told me! You may feel a bit surprised at this, but think first, have you ever asked your dad where he went to school? No? Well, neither had I.

"But you're not magic," I blurted before I could stop myself.

"Thanks."

"I mean..."

"I know what you mean, Trix. We can't do magic south of the border. Anyway, I've forgotten everything I learnt in school."

"So this, um, *cup*? Where is it?"

"I think," said Dad, looking at me mischievously, "I think, it's at Conundrums."

"Then why don't you go and get it?"

Then there was a lot of pausing and scratching his head and muttering about it being a long story and he didn't know if he should tell me and so on... But eventually I wheedled and wheedled until he told me the lot. My ears were on stalks, you can bet.

It turns out that in his younger years Dad had been a bit of a dreamboat. Well, he does have nice curly hair and witchy eyes, and I suppose they were curlier back then (his hairs, not his eyes). It also turns out that when he was sixteen, a young witch called Tabitha Tumultitude had been madly badly in love with him and they had gone out together for two years.

"Was she pretty?" I asked, feeling a bit odd and hot and jealous.

"She had eyes like stars – they came out at night," he joked. But then he said she was the most madly beautiful person he had ever seen.

"Oh," I said in a little small voice.

"But then I met someone who I loved much, much more, a sweet young teacher, called Edna Clump."

"Mum!" I said, feeling Very Extremely glad, but also a bit surprised.

"You don't understand, Trix, but your mum, with her nice ordinary family and her nice ordinary name and her nice solid teacher-training course, was the most glamorous person in my life. What did I want with witchy girls with long witchy hair and silvery skins?"

Well, you can't say fairer than that.

But when Dad broke the news to Tabitha, her head had started spinning round, she'd whirled and cursed ("Which only proves how right I was, Trix.") and used a particularly unpleasant plague-of-boils spell on him.

"The boils lasted for five years. Ugh. It was horrible."

"So that explains why the early photos always show you looking to one side? Was the other side of your face covered in BOILS?"

"Yes. And they were green, Trix. Not even the head of Conundrums could fix them."

Then Dad said it was the very same week that he broke the news to Tabitha that his precious *cup* went missing. He said he had always been sure that it was something to do with her, but there had been no way to prove it. She was a teacher herself now, at Conundrums.

"Why did they employ her after she'd covered you in boils?"

"Ah. Witches take love very seriously, Trixie, they think all's fair in love and war and they make exceptions for passionate crimes."

"But not stealing your *cup*, as well?"

"No one could prove it. Tabitha could make things disappear, you know. The vanishing spell is one of the most difficult spells of all to learn. I worked at it for years but could never manage it. Whenever I tried it, everything just went shiny."

"Shiny?"

"Yes, it always seemed to come out as the varnishing spell instead. I did have a pal who nearly mastered it. He made his quill pen vanish, and it did, all except the nib. It was tremendous seeing the nib writing all on its own. Of course, it is strictly forbidden to use the vanishing spell on living things, including, I am sorry to say, things attached to the living, like boils..."

"Dad," I said, Very Extremely seriously, "are you having me on?"

"Of course not, Trix. I'd never have told you any

of this if it wasn't for the fact that we're in such trouble and it's all my fault... You know your mum hates all the witchy side of the family."

It was true. And now I realised it was probably because of Tabitha. I would have hated them all too, if I had been Mum.

"But look, Dad, if your *cup* is at Conundrums, then you have to let me go on the course. I could get it! And save us all!"

"I know, I've been thinking the same thing," he said.

Right then, between us, I was sure we could persuade Mum. On the way home, Dad told me he'd do his best. "But if you DO find the *cup*, Trix, you must check it's mine. You don't want to be done for theft and Conundrums is bristling with trophies."

"But it'll have your name on it, won't it?"

"Yes, but these cups are magic. They're made of wizard's gold, don't laugh. The names only appear if you breathe on them gently. And – if you want me to persuade Mum to let you go – don't mention the *cup* again. OR Tabitha. OK?"

"It's a deal, Dad."

My luck was in. When we got home, there was another purple letter with gold handwriting and an owl stamp:

Conundrums Academy

Dear Trixie Tempest,

Please reply to our offer within two minutes of receiving this beemail, as demand for places on our half-term taster course exceeds supply.

Assuming your acceptance of our offer, bring with you the following, which may be ordered from Horrids, or are available at 10% discount for poorer pupils (slightly inferior quality), from Conundrums:

Simple Spells for Simple Minds (Book One)
Saucy Sorcery for Junior Wizards by Tabitha Tumultitude

Evil Doers' Guide (Elementary)
Potions
One warm cloak (colourways: indigo with silver stars, viridian with bronze stars, vermilion with gold stars)
Pointed hat (colourways as above)
Familiar

Yours faithfully,
Marcia Wince
Academy Secretary

"Familiar? What's that?"

"Oh you know, an owl, or a cat, or a snake," said Dad vaguely. "I had a dear little adder, used to follow me everywhere. Awfully good at adding, too."

"An adder?" said Mum. "You never told me."

"There are quite a lot of things I never told you," said Dad, winking at me.

Goodness. Perhaps he never told her about

Tabitha. Maybe he just pretended he had lost the *cup*? I wonder how he explained the boils? It was awfully nice of Mum to fall in love with a man covered in green boils all down one side.

"Oh Mum, I have to go, don't you see?" I said, smiling my most saddest, pleadingest, sweetest smile.

"Oh, Trix, you know we can't afford..."

But then Dad took Mum to one side. He said he was sure he could persuade Grandma Tempest to pay for the extras and what harm would it do and I'd be fed for a week and it would break my heart not to go. I don't know which of these things persuaded Mum to let me go – I'm afraid it was probably the free meals – but whatever. She said, as long as Grandma Tempest would cough up the dosh, I could go! Yes!

And I could take my best favourite of my dog Harpo's puppies, Bonzo, with me as my familiar! And I am the absolutely most extremely happy person in the whole wide world. Huzzaah!

But wait, it said reply in two minutes!

"Oh, that's just witches' nonsense," said Dad airily. "I'll get a beemail back to them today."

"What IS beemail? Is it sent by bees?"

Conundrums Academy
m o h t
t c m r
SCOTLAND

"Of course not," said Dad. "It's like email, only with paper."

"But this came by normal post!"

"Yes, they like to make it look like that, so as not to cause suspicion among the lower, I mean, ordinary people. Don't worry yourself about it. I promise I'll sort it out."

Mum gave Dad a Very Extremely beady look. She is always freaked out if he gets witchy.

"You promised me when we had the children you'd give all this up," she said.

"I have, I have, you know I have. This is different, this is for Trixie, just this once," he said, flashing his most winning smile. Probably the same smile that won the heart of mad old Tabitha...

And I had faith in Dad. I knew he could do it.

* * *

I charged to school, a Very Extremely happy person. Of course, Dinah and Chloe got all excited too.

"Surely there must be a way we could come." Dinah had her thinking cap on and you could almost see all the little cogs and springs in her head whirring about.

"Ooh, it's an awfully long way," worried Chloe.

"Wait, I know how we can go," said Dinah. "Why didn't I think of it before?"

What I was thinking was, she didn't think of it before because she hadn't needed to think of it before, had she? Before, she had thought it was all a joke. But what I said was, "What?"

"I have an aunt in Scotland! We can go and stay with her! Then I'll pretend you rang us up to spend a few days with you! Easy peasy lemon squeezy."

"Scotland's a very big place," moaned Chloe. Warty-Beak was amazed by how closely we were looking at our map all afternoon. Never mind that we were supposed to be looking at Africa or somewhere, we still looked like we were Very Extremely interested in our work and it must be nice for teachers, even ones with so few feelings as Warty-Beak, to think that their pupils are actually enjoying something.

And guess what? Dinah's auntie lived just five miles from Conundrums!

"We could walk it!" squeaked Dinah.

"But they'll never let us in," said Chloe, "to the gold mines."

"What are you talk—" I started, then realised Warty was hovering near.

Chloe and Dinah came back to mine for tea. Mum had made meringues. She was trying to make up for being rude the day before. We all pored over the letter and the lists from Conundrums.

"This is brilliant! We'll photocopy these and just change the names, so we've got one each," said Dinah. "We can make cloaks and stuff when we see yours, Trix."

"Well, I am not taking a familiar," said Chloe. "Unless I could take Bambi."

Bambi is her pet ant. Don't ask. Oh well, since you're interested, Chloe got one of those ant-farm thingies and had it in her bedroom and they all died except one which has been living for yonks. Well, about three weeks. But Chloe thinks she has had it for ever. She is a rather clingy person actually. She sometimes brings it to school in a matchbox.

"I don't think Bambi would count," said Dinah kindly. "And you might lose him."

"Well I couldn't leave him alone at home, could I?" wailed Chloe.

"Oh, shut up about Bambi!" Dinah got brutal. "You have a chance to go to Conundrums

Academy and you are going to turn it down for an ANT? Anyway, my aunt's got two pekes, we could take those, pretend it was a pets' sleepover or something."

"It won't work," said Chloe. "They'll never let us in."

And I had a pretty strong feeling she was right. But I was going, and, horrible as it may sound, that was good enough for me. To tell the truth, I was so excited I didn't really care if they came or not.

Chapter 3

Of course, I assumed Grandma T would cough up the dosh, and I was right. But it came with conditions:

"No running away," said Grandma T in her letter.

"Why on earth would I want to run away? She's bonkers," I said to Dad.

"She also says you have to pay the money back if you break anything or disgrace the name of Tempest," said Dad, trying to keep a straight face.

Lordy! But I was Happy As A Pig In Mud. (This is a saying of Grandma Clump's that I have never understood, like so many of Grandma Clump's sayings. Wouldn't a pig be happier in a nice cosy bed with a duvet? They're only happy in mud because that's all they've got.)

But happy as I was, and so excited I could hardly speak, as the day drew nearer I started having cold feet. What if I got homesick? I had heard of Year

Six kids getting homesick on school trips and having to sleep with the teacher. What if that happened to me? And I wouldn't know anyone at all...

Dinah's auntie had said Dinah and Chloe were welcome to come and stay. But I didn't think it was very likely they would be able to wangle themselves into Conundrums, after all, they do not have seventeen generations of witchy blood coursing through their veins. Still, we did have fun forging spell-book covers for them (which they put on old dictionaries), and making cloaks. The cloaks looked fantastic. I had already got mine: indigo with silver stars. It was the cheapest version and it was still amazerama, all shimmery and incredibly light and incredibly warm.

"It's real witchy material!" squeaked Chloe. "I wonder how they do it?"

We didn't do quite so well with our home-made ones, but we dyed a couple of old pairs of curtains viridian and vermilion and put gold stars on one and bronze stars on the other and they looked pretty good, not to boast or anything. Tomato helped with the dyeing. The vermilion didn't really change him that much, being such a round red person already, but the viridian was a sight to see.

"All we need is a sign saying GENUINE SPACE ALIEN FROM OUTER SPACE then we could put him in a cage and charge people 50p a look," said Dinah.

"I'm coming to Conundrums," squeaked Tomato. "Gonna be familiar."

"No Tom-Tom. You have to take an animal as your

familiar," I said kindly. I was feeling sorry for him, not going.

"Grrrrrrrr! Woof," he said.

I did wonder, as I'd had a few butterflies in my tummy the night before, whether I could disguise Tomato as a dog and smuggle him in with me, which shows how nervous I was getting. But I knew in my heart of hearts that it was going to be the most exciting place in the world and that when I was banqueting on witchy food and learning to ride a broomstick and all, whatever, I would forget about Dinah and Chloe and Tomato and everyone...

Needless to say, Chloe and Dinah insisted on staying the night with me the day before my big adventure. I wanted to be on my own really and I couldn't wait for the train journey. I could imagine the Conundrums Express, a proper scarlet steam train, probably leaving from platform seven and a half. My tickets said coach number thirteen, so that was a good start. At least that's what I tried to tell myself. I mean, I am not about to start Conundrums feeling superstitious. That's for ordinary folk, not clever witchy people.

"Ooh dear, coach thirteen," said Chloe cheeringly.

"Imagine a train with thirteen coaches, it'll be huge," said good old Dinah. "Destination: Highlands and Islands. Fab. Ooh, I do hope we can get there, by Wednesday at least?"

"No chance," said Chloe, and she looked really pleased. This was when I realised Chloe really didn't want to go to Conundrums at all. I suppose this was not surprising. I suppose Very Extremely shy, unadventurous types like Chloe do not jump about in excitement at the thought of broomstick rides and magical schools set in mountain wildernesses and all, whatever; they like them in books, but not in real life.

"You don't really want to come, do you Chloe?"

"Of course I do," she said, going the colour of Tomato.

Dinah shot me a look and I decided it was better to leave it.

"'Course you do," I said. "How's Bambi?"

And Chloe burst into tears. Apparently her mum had hoovered Bambi up that very morning.

"Ooh Chloe, you are brave not telling us," said Dinah.

I couldn't help wondering how she was sure it was Bambi who got vacuumed into the Hoover of Doom but I didn't like to ask, especially as Chloe was looking quite pleased at Dinah's praise. Dinah has that effect sometimes.

"He couldn't even have a proper funeral," stuttered Chloe. "We emptied the dust bag and went through it..."

"Yuk," said Dinah.

"But we couldn't find Bambi. So... so... I put all the dust in a shoe box and buried that."

Now you know I am sentimental – I mean, wasn't it me who campaigned to save the nit? – but even I thought an ant funeral was going a bit far.

"Got any marshmallows?" I asked.

"Loads," said Chloe. So we toasted them and talked about cloaks and spell books and Conundrums deep into the night.

Today's the day!

Chloe and Dinah slept like tops of course, but I

tossed and turned. I kept getting out of bed to check my packing.

1. Cloak
2. Hat
3. Spell books
4. Washbag
5. Underwear
6. Jeans
7. Tops
8. Paper and pens
9. Ten tins of Pooch-de-luxe for Bonzo
10. Dog biscuits
11. Trumpet (I never go anywhere without it)

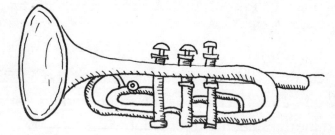

I kept feeling I'd forgotten something. I dropped off about dawn and was Very Extremely bleary-eyed when Mum came to wake us.

"You have packed your dressing gown?" she said.

I never wear a stupid dressing gown.

"You MUST," said Mum. "Conundrums is freezing at night time."

So we packed a moth-eaten old dressing gown from one of my witchy cousins.

"Why does it have such a long cord?" I asked.

"I expect they use it to lasso wild owls from their broomsticks," joked Mum.

And I'm Very Extremely glad she said that, as you will see later.

Dad was driving us to the station as Chloe and Dinah were keen to wave me off. (They weren't going up to Dinah's auntie's till the next day.) What with Tomato and Mum, and my bag, it was a bit of a squeeze, even in Dad's work van.

"What you got in there, Trix? The Tower of London?" said Mum, who had packed another whole bag of essentials like sticky plasters and lozenges and toothpaste and sandwiches for the journey. I wish she hadn't said that because

I felt I was being sent to the Tower of London at that point, to have my head cut off.

"Oh, Trix, you haven't packed your trumpet have you? They didn't say to take an instrument," said Dad.

"Well, I can practise in the evenings. I'll start a witchy band," I said. I take my trumpet everywhere.

The Tower of London feeling didn't improve when we lurched to a halt and tumbled out.

"Dad, this isn't the station," I said.

"It's the coach station," said Dad. "I'm afraid Grandma T didn't cough up quite enough for the train."

"She always was mean," muttered Mum.

"Oooh dear," said Chloe. "Coach thirteen, all on its own."

"Shut up," said Dinah, kicking her.

I could see immediately that this was just an ordinary coach full of ordinary people. I suppose all the other Conundrums pupils could afford the train... I was going to change my mind at that point but suddenly the coach was leaving and I was being bundled on. Dad thrust something into my hand. As he did so, he whispered to me, "No worries, Trix, but don't go near the wishing well. Promise?"

"You can stay half in and half out of the coach IF you like," bellowed the driver. "IF you want yer legs ripped off."

The last thing I remember seeing was Tomato's red face trying to kiss me through the window. I clutched Bonzo and waved merrily. It would be all right. It was only five days...

The coach racketed along. I was squashed between two women who smelt of cheese and a man the size of a rhino, who was snoring like a bulldozer.

He looked a bit like a bull dozing, actually. The seat in front had a red-haired boy about twelve, a bald thin pointy man who looked exactly like an egg on a peg and a woman who made a strange humming noise like a telly gone wrong. On the luggage rack there was an enormous barred cage with something snoring in it. It must be a very big dog, I thought, clutching Bonzo to me. I unwrapped Dad's parcel. It was the most beautiful quill pen, with a bright blue feather and what looked like a pure gold nib. It was inscribed:

"Tobias Terrapin Turtle Tempest, for good spell work, Conundrums Academy, Year Eight."

Terrapin? Turtle? Oh well, as long as no one at school finds out.

"Ooh, ain't that lovely," said Mrs Cheese. "That looks like a real witchy pen to me."

"It is," I said. (And by the way, I'm writing this book with that very pen now!)

"Hear that?" she said to Mrs Cheese Two. "She thinks it's a real witchy pen." And they both cackled. In fact, they were quite kind later and I discovered they smelt of cheese because they were on their way back from France with about six sackfuls of the stuff which they shared around the coach. Soon the whole coach smelt of cheese and it wasn't as nice as Cheesy Strings, I must say.

The Mrs Cheeses loved Bonzo and kept trying out cheeses on him. He seemed to like one called Brie the best, but unfortunately, what with that and the rickety old coach, he soon started looking green and we had to make an emergency stop for both of us to be sick. **The driver, who had been brought up somewhere near Hell, fumed about kids getting on without responsible adults.** It was not a Very Extremely good start to the journey. And what a long journey. We bumped and rattled and everyone moaned about the state of the roads and the coach's suspension and I noticed a little note Dad had put in with the pen:

Dear Trixie,

I haven't told Mum this, and I didn't want to worry you either. But Conundrums has one or two places in it I would advise you not to go to.

They are:

The wishing well

The forest out the back of the west wing (the little wood out the front by the east wing is fine)

The north tower

There is absolutely no reason why you should need to go to any of these, but if you should, make sure you go with a nice teacher.

Otherwise you will have an absolutely marvellous time, I know.

Keep the mobile charged!

Love Dad

What an exciting note. I really was in for an adventure, I knew it! But what did he mean, I wondered, by a nice teacher? Were any of the teachers at Conundrums like my own dear Warty-Beak? Surely not. Witches and wizards would be cool. There was a note from Mum and Tomato, too:

> Darling,
>
> Do ring if you need anything at all.
>
> Eat well. Don't stay up too late!
>
> Tons of love,
>
> Mumxxxxx
>
> MISS YOU LUV
> TOMATO xxxxxxxxxxxxxxxxxxxx
> xxxxxxxxxxxxxxxxxxxxxxxxxxx

so of course I felt disgustrously homesick.

"Ooh, are you feeling poorly again, dear?" said Mrs Cheese One. "Have a peppermint."

The peppermint was a good idea. It was so hot, it took off the roof of my mouth, and I stopped moping and dozed off.

When I woke up, Bulldozer had gone (how he squeezed past me without waking me up I'll never know), the Mrs Cheeses were snoozing and the boy with the red hair had Bonzo on his lap and was reading to him from *Just William*. Goodness, I'd never thought of reading to the puppies. Maybe if we read to baby animals they would grow up Very Extremely clever like us and start ruling the world. I think a world ruled by dogs would be a nicer place than this one, as it happens, with lots of parks everywhere and loos on every corner and no school.

I realised I had slept for four hours and soon me and the boy, who was called, by the humming woman, Bartholomew, but told me that his mum was mad and his real name was Bart, were sharing our sandwiches.

"I'm going to witch school," he said.

"Shhhhhh!" said Eggpeg. "Don't talk nonsense." Then he added, trying to smile at me, "He has a very vivid imagination."

"Ooh," I whispered. "So am I."

"Don't be daft," he said, quite kindly. "You can't go till you're much bigger."

I sometimes forget I am knee high to an ant.

"I am ten and three-quarters, as it happens," I said, in a sophisticated voice, "and I am going for a half-term taster course. Why are you going in half-term, anyway?"

"Oh, Conundrums terms are completely different from ordinary schools," he said. "Only most people have started two weeks ago."

He looked glumly at his shoes, which I noticed were bright green with pointy toes.

"What's it like? Do you like it?" I added, seeing he was looking far from jolly.

"It's a long story," he said. Then, "Look, there it is!"

And I turned to look out at the misty mountains. There, rising from the mist, was a huge building that looked like a cross between a cathedral and a castle. It had loads of different towers and domes and one Very Extremely huge steeple covered in gold. I was gobsmacked. It was even better than I

had imagined. When you have been going to a school that looks like an oversized egg carton, this is the kind of place you sometimes dream of. Well, I do.

"Bartholomew, stop annoying the little girl and come and annoy us," said the humming woman. I tried to tell them that I liked talking to Bart, but they were those sort of parents who do not listen to any

children and they yanked poor Bart to sit with them.

"You know you are NEVER to talk about school to ordinary folk!" hissed Eggpeg.

"But she's going there, too," squeaked Bart. "Aren't you?"

"Yes," I said.

"Nonsense, you're far too young," was all the answer I got.

And suddenly the driver was shouting out my stop: "Brigadoon."

The Cheeses and us were the only people left on the coach. They pressed a bag of cheese and peppermints on me as I got off, although I will never ever eat cheese again for the whole of my life.

I noticed Bart looking miserably back at me as his parents rushed him off towards a fantastic looking coach pulled by four enormous horses. Bart had the huge cage with him. It must be his familiar. What on earth could it be?

I stumbled after them. A Very Extremely cold thin rain was falling. Was I supposed to get in the coach with Bart? I had been told a driver would pick me up, but I wasn't prepared for a Conundrums driver.

"Trixie Tempest?" said a voice that sounded like a horse whinnying. I looked round.

"Well, are you Trixie Tempest or not?" neighed the voice.

"Come on, get in," shouted Bart.

"Chaff and mangles!" came the voice again. "Don't they teach these half-termers anything?"

And then I realised that it was one of the horses who was talking to me. I froze. This was too much magic. I knew then that I was completely unprepared for this. In my heart of hearts I had really expected Conundrums to be a cosy sort of conjuring trick school and now I was being taken to a gold-plated castle by talking horses.

"Oh, come on, dear," said a kinder voice. I think it was the horse on the left at the back, but my knees were trembling and I couldn't seem to make my legs do what they should. "Don't you like horses?"

"I LOVE horses," I squeaked. "They're my favourite animals!"

"Well, in you get then, we want an early night."

So in I got. And that was just the start.

Chapter 2

Bart, Eggpeg and Hum were completely silent on the journey to Conundrums. The only sound as we wound through the misty woods (or was it the forest Dad had said don't go to?) was the jingle of harness, the snoring and rattling of the huge cage, the wet clopping of the horses' hooves and the occasional complaint from the driver, who was the grumpy horse who had first spoken to me. "Cobblestones and bits! They should clear this path up! This is four stallions' work!" and so on.

I realised I must be dreaming and would soon wake up in my cosy bed. I know you must think it sounds exciting, but I was knackered and Very Extremely nervous. I hated Eggpeg and Hum. How could they be so unfriendly? And poor old Bart was just gazing at his luminous green elfy shoes.

Then there was an ear-splitting noise. "GRRRR RRRAOOOOOOWR" I jumped out of my skin and back into it so fast you wouldn't know I'd been away.

"What was THAT?" I croaked, gazing at the cage, which was now shuddering and shaking as something seemed to be scratching at it furiously.

"Oh, just Flossie," said Bart. "She'll be all right when we get there. I hope."

Eggpeg and Hum shot him a look that would have frozen a polar bear. But then, we jolted to a halt. I looked up to see Conundrums Castle looming high above us, lights shining out of hundreds of windows. My stomach lurched. It really did exist then. Obviously, JK Rowling had been here herself, but just pretended she was making it all up. But why hadn't she mentioned the talking horses?

Now I was really excited. There would be a magic banquet, obviously. And I was starving. As long as I avoided wishing wells and forests and the north tower and nasty teachers (Dark Arts teachers, obviously), I would be just fine. And then I thought of Bart's red hair.

"Your name isn't Weasley, is it?" I asked.

"Oh, not another one," huffed Eggpeg.

"That's all fairy tales," said Hum, easing the now growling, shuddering cage out of the coach. I hoped whatever was inside wouldn't get out.

Bart gave me a sad smile and said, "See ya."

"But I'm coming too!" I shouted, struggling to get out.

"Not half-termers!" neighed the driver. "Little pip-squeaks like you go to the apprentices' school. Whatever next?" And the coach swept off, and I was alone, except for Bonzo.

We plodded on listening to the moaning horses. Moan, moan, moan. I had always dreamt of a talking horse, but all they talked about was the cost of hay, the state of the roads, how they never got enough oats, how the harness hurt, how it was a waste of horsepower sending four horses for one half-termer and a truant. It was even more boring than adults. It was getting dark and I was just wondering again if maybe this was the forest, not the wood, when we came to a little clearing and stopped.

"Out you get," snorted the driver.

I stumbled out in front of a little ramshackle building that looked a bit like St Aubergine's only grottier. If you have been to St Aubergine's you will know that it is quite hard to look grottier than that.

"Good luck," said the nice horse, who was a gorgeous palomino, like Merlin, the horse-of-my-dreams that I aim to own one day.

"Thanks," I said. It was the first kind word I'd had since the Cheeses.

"If you need anything," said the horse, "just call for Merlin, that's me."

Merlin! He was called Merlin! The horse-of-my-dreams could talk! I immediately started planning how I could persuade him to come home with me; it would be much nicer for him than being with this grumpy lot pulling witches' coaches. But my dream was interrupted by the gloomy driver.

"Is that all?" he hissed. "No tip?"

"Oh," I said, fumbling around in my bag. I only had a five pound note with me 'for emergencies'. But of course Mum had packed some apples. I took out a big red one.

"There are four of us." So that was all my apples gone except one.

I walked nervously up to the door, and was just about to knock, when it swung open as if by, well, magic.

I was expecting a big room, because I was convinced by now that although this place looked ordinary from the outside, it would be much bigger inside, but there was a little pokey corridor with a little pokey witch standing there rubbing her hands. She looked just like a witch out of a story – about 900 years old, all warts and fingernails and pointy hat.

"Welcome to my gingerbread house," she squawked. "Just a little joke," she added, glancing at my face, which I could feel had the nervous look of a Very Extremely nervous person. "Been on our half-term taster before? No? Come and register."

I put down all my details: name, age, qualifications, school and town.

"Bottomley!" she squealed, as though it was the funniest thing she'd ever heard. I thought witches were more grown-up than that. When I am a grown-up I think I will say I was brought up in Paris, or Barbados, or somewhere respectable.

"I'm Madam Mope, the housekeeper," she said. "Don't expect much from me, because I'm paid in turnips. If turnips is what you get, turnips is what you give." And she stumped off up the pokey staircase to show me my room.

My heart sank. I had expected a big jolly dormitory full of loads of bouncy young witches. But it was a room the size of a nit's suitcase. A bigger person simply could not have fitted into it and there wasn't room for me and Madam Mope at the same time. The peeling walls were a dismal mouldy mushroom colour and the bed looked as if it was made of matches. That was the only thing, apart from a three-legged stool, in the room. There were no curtains and it was freezing. Even Bonzo whimpered at the sight of it.

"Of course, you can change the decor, it's up to you," she wheezed.

"But I haven't got any paint, or bedclothes."

"Paint!" she chortled. "Bedclothes! Hee-haw heeeeee! You do it by magic! You'll soon learn. That's what they thrive on here, you know. Treat 'em mean, keep 'em keen! Heh heh. Hope you've got something for the pooch," she said, glancing at Bonzo for the first time. "Extras aren't included, unless you've got a proper familiar. I'll let you settle in. Washing's down the corridor to the left. Lessons start at 6.30 sharp. Breakfast at 6.00. Be sure to read the rule book. And this," she pointed at Bonzo, "has to be put in the kennels first thing with all the other familiars." And she was gone.

Luckily I had brought Bonzo's bowl. He wolfed down two tins of Pooch-de-luxe, but I was starving. Obviously, I had missed supper. It was ten o'clock. The bathroom was about the size of my room, but nothing worked. The light was on, but it was about as bright as a candle, and no water came out of the taps.

And the loo didn't flush. Oh no. I tried and tried but it wouldn't work. It didn't even make that cranky sound ours does, you know the sort of thing, a promise of a flush, a hopeful gurgle. It is Very Extremely embarrassing being in a strange house when you can't flush the loo. Well, after about eighteen goes I decided that no one would know it was me. So I started off to bed. But just as I was leaving the bathroom a watery voice like

someone from the depths of the sea, gurgled:
"FLUSH ME."

I could not believe my lugholes. A talking loo.

"FLUSH ME," it commanded again.

"I'm trying to!"

So I tried another twenty-five billion times and nothing happened. I do not cry as you know, and I have no idea why my cheeks were wet, since there wasn't a drop of water in that bathroom, but I think sometimes your eyes can water, if you are very tired and haven't eaten anything and you meet a talking lavatory.

So I tried to leave the room again.

"FLUSH ME."

I do not want to bore you and drive you to reading books about ballet or something, so I'll just say this happened about six more times and then I DID leave and slammed the door.

And I could hear **"FLUSH ME, FLUSH ME, FLUSH ME, FLUSH ME,"** all the way down the corridor to my room.

But I had escaped! I can deal with a talking loo. I can't deal with a walking loo, though, and just to be sure it wasn't going to follow me I pushed the three-legged stool against the door and wedged it under the handle. With the door shut I could still hear **"FLUSH ME"** very faintly, but I had a happy thought: the Mrs Cheeses. I rummaged around in my bag. Cheese and peppermints. Yummy. This only goes to show that when you make a resolution such as, "I will never ever eat cheese again for the whole of my life," you can forget to keep it after only a few hours. So what hope is there for the tweenagers of the world to keep their rooms tidy, do their homework on time and all, whatever?

I ate something called Gorgonzola, which looked very disgustrous but tasted lovely with peppermints. I think I will be a chef when I grow up, specialising in Cheesy Strings, marshmallows, Gorgonzola and peppermints. But marshmallows only made me think of Chloe, and that made me think of home.

I'll just ring them, for a chat, I thought. But I had promised myself I wouldn't. I was not going to be one of those wimps who call home at the slightest thing. I mean, what had happened; a couple of bossy horses and a bossy loo and a witch as old as time who doesn't give you a duvet. There were worse things in life. And if it all got worse, I could always phone in the morning.

I put on both my jumpers and my socks and my dressing gown to go to bed because there was only one sheet. The bed was not made of matches, in fact, it was made of pebbles. The pillow was made of much bigger rocks.

The wind howled through the cracks in the windowsill and the rain dripped through a few holes in the roof. But I was so tired I dropped off straight away and slept like a twig. Adults have often told me that cheese late at night gives you nightmares. Another grown-up porky pie.

"Good morning, good morning, good morning, another lovely day, But rain or shine it's always fine on your half-term taster stay."

This disgustrous jingle woke me up at 5.45 a.m. It seemed to be sung by a hyena and certainly not someone who knew any notes of actual music. I leapt out of bed, fully dressed, pulled my cloak on, stuffed my mad wig up into my hat because I couldn't find my hairbrush and legged it straight downstairs, Bonzo under one arm. I was starving.

I charged into the dining room and stopped dead. There was a long table with two rows of girls. Some of them were about five and the oldest looked about thirteen and they were all identically dressed in white smocks and with white ribbons in their hair. They all looked up at me at once and a giggle ran round the room.

"Someone hasn't read the rule book," said a long thin girl with plaits, who reminded me horribly of Grey Griselda.

"I didn't know there was... a... uniform," I muttered.

"It's under your pillow," said Madam Mope. "I TOLD you last night."

I tore upstairs and sure enough, under my pillow – if you could call it a pillow – were: two starched white smocks, two white hair ribbons, two pairs of green tights and a pair of the green pointy shoes that Bart had been wearing. And a Very Extremely fat book called Conundrums Rule Book: Half-term Taster Edition.

Yuk. I hate school uniforms. I think they are a horrendous way of making you feel you are not a person, but this was the pits. A smock! No trousers! Hair ribbons! This was not my scene at all, I can tell you. But I was so starving I thought I could complain later – and, to be honest, I did want to fit in. It had not been a Very Extremely nice feeling having everyone giggling at me. I expect it has happened to you, so you know what I mean.

As for the rule book, I couldn't believe how fat it was. I like reading, it is one of the few things at school I am any good at, but I didn't see how I could wade through that in just five days...

There was no mirror in my room, but I could tell the uniform was about twice my size. I waddled down the corridor in my stupid elf shoes, feeling like a frog in fancy dress, and tried to slip unnoticed into the dining hall.

"This is Trixie Tempest, it's her first half-term taster course, so be nice to her. NO practical jokes," said the Mope, busily clearing away the plates. "I've kept it warm for you, since it's your first day," she said to my relief. "I'll take that to the kennels," and she whisked poor old Bonzo away. Then she served me up a dish of something that looked exactly like, well I don't like to say, but, well, vomit. It smelt like old socks. It tasted like old trainers. It made you think longingly of school dinners. Even in my starving state I couldn't eat much.

Twenty-seven heads turned to look at me and fifty-four little rows of teeth like sharks all roared with merry laughter. I was sure they hadn't all eaten this disgustrous stuff. Obviously they knew something I didn't but they weren't going to tell me what.

There were still five minutes to lessons and everyone was gabbling away to each other; obviously they all knew each other already.

"Have you been here before?" I asked the girl next to me. Her eyes widened like saucers.

"Of course! We've all been coming since we were five. You're the first new girl *ever*," she said snootily. "Top group is going to the Academy next year." She looked down her long nose at me and turned to her friend, giggling.

"Aren't there any boys?" I dared to ask, thinking of Bart.

"Boys! Euk!" she snorted. "We don't have to be with the boys until sixth form. Boys are in north and south wings and girls are in east and west wings. You want to watch out, you do. You get put in the stocks if you talk to a boy."

Obviously, this was a dream. I decided to relax and just see where it would take me. I'd wake up soon, in my cosy bed at home, with Tomato and all the puppies.

"Lessons!" snapped Mope.

Everyone jumped to their feet and stood behind their chairs like robots.

"Thank you for this lovely food.

Forgive those of us who were rude,"

they chanted, looking directly at yours truly when they said "rude".

Lovely food? Were they mad? Come back Orange Orson, Grey Griselda and Warty-Beak, all is forgiven, I thought.

Everyone picked up their spell books and filed out, with me trailing behind.

The timetable said:

6.30 a.m. Spelling. Teacher: Madam Manky

"Good better best,
Never let it rest,
Till your good is better
And your better BEST."

A long streak in a snowy cape and snowy witchy hat was chanting this as we entered. At St Aubergine's everyone would have laughed their heads off, but these girls all looked very solemn and sat down in neat rows opening their books as though they were one person. Then they all chanted back:

"Spell spell well,

Well well spell,

We cannot be happy till we've learnt to SPELL."

It was beginning to feel a bit like church. I've only been to church twice as it happens: once was a Very Extremely nice carol service when I was about five, and the other was with Dinah's family and was all kneeling and standing like yo-yos, and I was always up when I should have been down and didn't know the words.

"Welcome half-termers!" sang Madam Manky. "We are so sorry to have lost three of you, it is the first time our taster course has been reduced from thirty young witches, but we are delighted to welcome the new girl, Miss Tempest. Stand up, Tempest, oh, I see you are standing up."

Cue for more giggles. Well, you try being knee high to an ant and see how you like it.

"Now, Tempest, can you spell frogspawn?"

"F – R – O—" I stuttered, because I wasn't sure whether the spawn bit was spelled like "born" or not and I was worried about getting to the end. Spelling is not my strong point, although as you can see, I am Very Extremely good at writing, not to boast or anything. But everyone was laughing at me now. Why? Surely I hadn't got frog wrong?

"No, no, dear," trilled the loony Manky, "this is *Spelling*. Don't laugh girls, poor Tempest has been to an *ordinary* school, she is not lucky like all of you. At *ordinary* schools they are still learning to spell quite simple words at your age, amazing though it might sound. Now Tempest, you have heard of frogs turning into princes, I expect?"

89

I nodded.

"Well, frogspawn is just a very elementary spell, along the same lines. Tumbleweed, show her how."

Tumbleweed was the snooty girl in plaits. She swept up to the front of the class, waved her hand over Manky's water glass and, wow! It was seething with frogspawn. "There! Excellent, Tumbleweed, a whole jar of little baby princelings, who knows? One for each of you if you spell well. So, Tempest, just listen along today and see if you can catch up a bit later by Burning the Midnight Oil."

Well, I don't mind saying, but snooty or not, I was impressed by the frogspawn thingy. I decided I would work Very Extremely hard.

"Our spell for

today is on page 244: a very useful little spell for white teeth. I can see you've all done your homework," she said gazing at the rows of little sharky numbers.

Great, I thought, no more tooth brushing if I can master this.

"Is there one for hair brushing?" I asked.

"Certainly, dear, for those who need it. It's on page 608."

Sure enough, there it was. This could be Very Extremely handy if you could get all this stuff done and have more time to play.

I tried really hard with the tooth thingy, which involved pointing at each tooth, then stroking each one with a feather and muttering a spell. "No helping" was the rule, so I tried to watch what Tumbleweed and the others were doing. I was pretty sure I had it right and I could see everyone else's teeth were even sparklier than before. All this whiteness was giving me a bit of headache by now, what with the smocks and the ribbons and all.

Then Manky marched down the lines inspecting everyone. "Marvellous, Tumbleweed; excellent, Baker; superb, Dankworth."

What weird names, I was thinking, until I remembered she had called me Tempest and I realised they were just using second names, like the army.

"Ah, Tempest. Aaaaah. Um, would you like to smile for the class?"

Well, I tried. I've never got such a laugh as that and I am a bit of a joker. Manky whipped out a mirror and even I had to laugh when I saw myself. I'd thought my teeth had gone black, but actually every one was a different coloured pattern.

The girl next to me suddenly gave me a really nice smile. "How d'you DO that?" she said. "You look like a rainbow."

"Oh, it was nothing," I muttered.

Manky flapped her hand and chanted, "Colours bright back to white," and my teeth went back to their usual mix of yellow and beige, like everyone else's (in the *ordinary* world, that is). Oh well, I thought, all this pointing and feathering and muttering is harder work than brushing them, so what's the point?

Sport was next: I had to wear a spare PE kit that was white shorts and a vest with a Conundrums logo and FRILLS. I was feeling like a bit of running about but there were only six of us, not enough for football.

"Where is everyone?" I asked Barnstaple, the nice girl who'd said I looked like a rainbow.

"Oh, everyone skives off PE to practise nail-varnishing spells," she said. "The teachers don't mind, because they don't expect girls to do sport." What a weird idea!

The sports mistress, Madam Sprint, was exactly like an apple, round and rosy.

"What shall we do today?" she said. And I thought I'd found a nice teacher at last. Wrong.

I put my hand up. "Can we play Snarg?" I was desperate to learn about it.

Usual gales of laughter.

"We don't do Snarg, er, Tempest, it's for boys."

Lordy! At least at St Aubergine's girls are

allowed to play football if they want to.

"But there are only six of us – couldn't we have a go?"

The apple turned into a lemon. "I think you heard what I said," she snapped. "Cold shower for insubordination."

"Ooooh," hissed Barnstaple.

"Take her, Barnstaple. And DON'T let her off."

So Barnstaple took me to the shower room which was a corrugated tin hut.

"If you promise not to tell," she whispered, "I'll take the chill off it, otherwise you'll freeze. A girl last year lost the end of a finger with frostbite."

"WHAT? I'm not going in," I shouted.

"It'll be worse if you don't," she said. And I could see she meant it. "Thing is, at Conundrums you're never supposed to talk back to teachers," said Barnstaple, pushing me gently towards the shower.

Ever swum in a lake in winter? I have and this was colder.

"I th-th-th-thought you said you'd take th-th-th-the ch-ch-ch-chill off," I stuttered when she let me out.

"I DID," Barnstaple protested. "You'd know if you'd had one before."

When I staggered back to the sports field in one piece, Madam Sprint looked surprised. "Hmmm, Tempest, you're tough meat, I see."

I hate to say it, but I felt flattered. I suppose this is how torturers keep people in their power.

There were about twenty minutes of sport left and we played Bumble Bee, which is a bit like Donkey, only we were throwing a

Disgustrous P.E. Kit with FRILLS

ball which had a mind of its own and you had to make friends with it to make it go in the right direction. It was fun and by the end I was calling Barnstaple Barney. I had a friend.

But at lunch time things went really wrong.

My food was a plate of soggy mush again, like in *Oliver Twist*. And everyone else had roast chicken and chips!

"Why have I got this?" I asked Barney.

"Oh, you have to do a spell to make it change," she said. "But you have to learn it, I'm afraid we're not allowed to help."

"Can you make it turn into anything you like? I'm a veggie," I whispered.

"Oh, I don't know, they've only told us roast chicken, roast beef and roast lamb so far, but you get veggies with it. Then there's pudding spells, too."

"But you must help me, please, I've no idea," I pleaded.

She looked nervous. "It's against the rules. You should have done your homework."

It got worse. They all had trifle and I had another plate of the same.

"But yours is coming out like trifle! You're not doing anything to change it!"

"You say your food spells first thing in the morning," whispered Barney. "Read the rule book."

"Ooh, Barnstaple, got a new friend now the baddies have left?" squealed Tumbleweed. "Better not let HER get you into trouble or you'll be out on your ear."

Barney blushed.

"What's that all about?" I asked.

"It's a long story," she muttered.

The day got worse. There were tests in every subject and, of course, yours truly failed them all. I have never been Very Extremely good at Maths, but Magic Maths, which you would think would be there to make life easier, was like a mad house.

You only had to say multiply and you got zillions of little numbers pouring out of your pen! If you thought subtract in the wrong way, everything you'd written down would vanish!

"More discipline, Tempest!" shrieked the Maths teacher, who had a long orange face exactly like a carrot. I realised pretty soon that food was the only thing I could think of.

Conundrums Academy was turning out to be so Very Extremely NOT what I was expecting. And all the spells were about making yourself look nice. Or cleaning up and making your house look nice. How boring is that? Very Extremely boring, that's how. Even poor old Bonzo's spirits were low, as I discovered when we had the Familiar-training Course. He was so pleased to see me he shot out of the cage into my arms.

"Tempest!" shouted Madam Brute, who looked, not to be rude, like a gorilla only not as friendly. "Control your familiar!"

"He's only a puppy," I stuttered.

"Then he is unsuitable for this course," she fumed. "Didn't anyone tell you?"

I looked around at all the other familiars, who were sitting in a neat line. Well, if you could call a line that included five owls, two frogs, eight cats, six lizards, three snakes, a badger, a hawk and a Dalmatian, neat.

"Now, Tempest and, and..."

"Bonzo," I said, while everyone sniggered.

"Bonzo. You just watch and hopefully you will learn enough to participate towards the end of the week."

So I got a good cuddle with Bonzo, which I needed. I hoped he wasn't getting the same food I was.

But the Familiar-training Course was the best thing of the day. It was amazing. All the animals did everything they were told! It was like they'd been hypnotised! It 's hard enough for me to get old Harpo to "sit" or "fetch", but this lot, even the frogs, did somersaults on command.

"We're teaching them to fly when we go up to the Academy," whispered Barney, proud of her frog, who had just pole-vaulted over an Olympic-style hurdle.

"What? The frogs?"

"And the cats. And the dogs. And the birds have to learn how to eat with knives and forks."

Well, I was beginning to think anything was possible. But I had a burning question.

"None of the loos seem to be working. D'you know if someone is fixing them?"

"So it was YOU," she said. I don't think she meant to shout but of course Tumbleweed tumbled up.

"What's she done now?" she asked.

"Um," said Barney.

"Don't protect her, Barney, you know what happens if you're too helpful."

"All I said is why weren't the loos working," I said defiantly.

"So it was YOU," Tumbleweed shouted, as loudly as possible. "I might have known. Hey everyone, it was Tempest that didn't flush."

Well, I was flushing now, for sure.

"She probably doesn't know the spell."

"She's useless."

"I don't know why they let these *ordinary* girls in. They're such a bore."

"She doesn't even know the hair-brushing spell, obviously. Don't they brush their hair out there in the ordinary world?" added Tumbleweed. And then everyone joined in.

"Or clean their teeth?"

"Or flush their loos?"

"Or take a bath?"

"And are they all as weedy as you?"

"And do they all have little smelly puppies? Euk."

I'd like to say it was the insulting of Bonzo that set me off, or the lack of food, or being homesick, but whatever it was, I saw scarlet and the famous witchy Tempest temper took hold and I launched myself at Tumbleweed, and grabbed her plaits, and pretty soon we were rolling around on the grass and all the familiars went berserk.

Next thing I knew I was being dragged off Tumbleweed by four owls and a hawk. All squawking like loonies (well, like birds, I suppose) and flapping their wings so hard I thought they would fly off with me. I wish they had, because towering over me was the vast figure of Madam Brute.

"Stocks," was all she said.

Look, you're not going to believe this, but Brute dragged me off and put me in the stocks. Honest, those horrible old wooden things that you've probably seen in fairgrounds or old castles, or you might have had a teacher kind or silly enough to sit in one while you pelt them with wet sponges at the school fair.

They put my head and arms in one set of holes and my legs in another, and I struggled and demanded my rights and all, whatever and it was no good. I had to stay locked in there for three whole hours, until supper time and every now and then someone would sneak out of a lesson and call me smelly. And next to me was a red-haired sobbing girl who said she had been in there ALL DAY and she didn't know when she would be let out. She said her name was Damp but she couldn't really talk, because she was crying all the time.

Well, that was it for me. I was going to take the first coach or bicycle or bus straight back home. I hated them all. Even Barney hadn't tried to save me.

* * *

Madam Mope came creaking out to unlock me at 7 p.m.

"I hope you've learnt your lesson," she said.

I was too tired to argue. "I'm ringing my parents to tell them about this and to ask to go home," was all I said.

"No, dear, they signed the paper. There is no way out of Conundrums until the course is over. Look," she said, more kindly, as we were walking back, "it's more than my job's worth to say this, but this place isn't what it was in the old days. Things have got much tougher here. If you'd read the rule book, like I told you, you would have known. Girls often get homesick, but there's no escape, I'm afraid. Just do what you're told and it will soon be over."

That's what you think, I thought. I knew I had Dad's trusty mobile. But of course, as soon as I got to my room, I found it didn't work. The batteries were OK, but there was no reception. And that was my Darkest Hour. No Dinah, no Chloe, no parents. No Tomato. Gruel. Stocks. Freezing showers. Disgustrously boring spells. I had to plan my escape. But how?

Then I thought, THE *CUP*. That's what I'd come here for, and I was determined to get it now, whatever happened. That was my task and I was going to get it come hell or high water.

I missed supper, I couldn't face everyone. Instead, I made a little nest out of my pillow and sheet and snacked on peppermints and cheese while I read the rule book and *Simple Spells for Simple Minds*.

There were three things I had to learn in order to survive: loo flushing, tap turning and food spells. I practised them all for about three hours, then I tiptoed down the corridor to try out the loo. The first time, it just gurgled and spat. But on about the fourth time it worked! You may feel it's a bit pathetic, being so pleased you can flush a loo, but I felt it was important to keep my self-respect, because that is all I had left.

Then I tried the tap turning and it worked first time! I didn't want to risk a bath just yet, I thought it might start shouting at me, so I washed all over but then I couldn't get the tap to turn off. I realised I hadn't looked that bit up. I couldn't bear to ask for help so I just pulled the plug out, hared back to my room, looked up how to turn it off, hared back – and it worked. I felt that great feeling you have when your luck is changing for the better, although if it hadn't been for the *cup* I would have flooded the place, happily.

I fell asleep about halfway through reading the rule book. I kid-you-not, it was like reading about medieval torture back in the dark ages. Rule after rule after rule – and this was just a half-term taster! Why did anyone want to go to Conundrums?

Surely magic wasn't worth this kind of pain?

Chapter 5

I'd been practising the food spell as I fell asleep. I couldn't wait to try it. I was going to turn my breakfast gruel into scrambled eggs, toast and honey and Krispy Popsickles.

Fat chance. All I got was an uncooked sausage. Veggies can eat raw sausage if they're starving, I told myself, looking round. But now nobody  was speaking to me at all, even Barney, who had her peepers glued to the table.

Mope creaked in: "The new girls arrived half an hour ago. They're just settling into their rooms so we will be up to twenty-nine again, and if Damp is released, perhaps we shall be able to have a full class again," she announced.

Ten minutes later, just as I was deciding it was an uncooked sausage or nothing, a wonderful thing happened. Everyone cheered as two figures – a long thin one and a short round one – shuffled in, their heads bowed. And with them were two little familiars: Pekingeses! YES!

"This is Dare-deVille and Caution, who seem excellent students and have read the rule book before they came," said Mope, glaring at yours truly.

I was just about to fling myself into their arms when I caught the look on Dinah's face, which would have frozen hell over with ice to spare. Obviously, she had a Plan. And that Plan meant, don't say you know me.

All the snooty girls bombarded them with questions:

"What school do you go to?"

"How many houses have you got?"

"What kind of car?"

"You mean your school is FREE? How absolutely ghastly. You'd better sit with Tempest."

"SHE goes to a free school," said Dinah, in a brilliant fake posh voice. "But I go to Lah-de-dah College for gentlefolk. Which is almost as good as Conundrums Academy."

Hah! Chloe was looking really annoyed, but Detective Tempest could tell Dinah was trying to get in with the snooties.

We had ten minutes free time before lessons and I managed to sneak them both into my room.

"This place is hell," said Dinah grumpily. "They've given us revolting uniforms, a book of rules bigger than the bible and beds made of concrete."

"We've killed ourselves getting here," added Chloe. "Why didn't you warn us?"

"The mobile's dead. It's a prison," I said and told them everything.

"Stocks?" Chloe's eyes were saucers on stalks.

"It's even worse than I thought. We have to escape," said Dinah.

"We might get caught," said Chloe.

"I've got to get that *cup*," I said. "And guess what? Look at tomorrow's timetable." I showed them:

Cup and sorcery demonstration by Year Thirteen Conundrums tutor, Tabitha Tumultitude.

"See? It's *her*," I said.

"Who?" they said. They have memories like sieves.

"*Her.* Tabitha Tumultitude." They still looked blank. "The witch who stole the *cup* from Dad!"

"Oh. So?"

"So let's trap her."

"Mmmmmmmmm," said Dinah. "I can feel a Plan coming on..."

At lunch, Dinah turned on the charm. "Oh, I LOVE your hair," she said to Tumbleweed. "Is that a variation on the hair-brush spell? I can't even do the basic one. I'm hopeless. But you're just brilliant." Then she whispered, "I think you're the cleverest witch here, and the prettiest."

Tumbleweed blushed! Dinah can be very charming.
Then Dinah asked innocently, gazing at her gruel.
"Can you do anything except chicken and chips?"

"Of course," said
Tumbleweed, tossing
her disgustrous braids.
"Anything."

"Oh, go on, just this
once, you don't have to show
me how, so it's not helping me,"
wheedled Dinah.

"What would you like?" said Tumbleweed.

And then Dinah did something Very Extremely
kind. I could see she was dying for chicken and
chips, but she said "nut roast".

Everyone shrieked with laughter.

"Yuk," said Tumbleweed. "Never tried that. Still,
I suppose if you're a veggie... Shall I do it? Just this
once?"

"Yes!" they all shouted.

"Only if all the new girls don't look," said
Tumbleweed.

So me and Dinah and Chloe got blindfolded.
And about a minute later there was a steaming

plate of macaroni cheese on Dinah's plate. Tumbleweed looked quite surprised herself.

"Oooh, Tumbleweed," said all the little witchkins. "We've never done macaroni cheese!"

"Wow!" said Chloe.

Even Dinah was impressed. "You're a genius," she said to Tumbleweed, shovelling the macaroni over to me. Well, she had eaten only last night and I was starving, but even so it was more than kind.

"I didn't mean it for worm!" said Tumbleweed. So Dinah wheedled her into chicken and chips for her and Chloe.

"Only just this once. It's against the rules," said Tumbleweed. And Dinah went on buttering her up in such a revolting way that we got strawberry ice cream with wafers, too. I  felt happy for the first time for days.

"Now, tell us about this Tabitha Tumultitude," said Dinah.

"Oh, she's the queen of Conundrums," sighed Tumbleweed.

"You mean the head teacher?"

"'Course not. But everyone there has a crush on her. She's head of Cup and Sorcery! She's an amazing witch. They say she can turn pebbles into meringues with whipped cream and glacé cherries on top." Everyone sighed. "And she's beautiful. Actually, people say I look like her."

"You do, you do," simpered all the little witchkins.

"Ooooh, she can't be as pretty as you, surely?" sighed Dinah.

Yuk. I wasn't sure it was worth being fed, all this disgustrous flattery.

"So, this Tabitha Tumultitude – she's absolutely perfect?" asked Dinah.

"Yes, yes," said the witchkins.

But Tumbleweed whispered something in Dinah's ear. "Don't tell the little ones," and Dinah winked at her.

"And we're actually going up to Conundrums Castle for her lesson?" Dinah continued.

"Yes, yes," chorused the witchkins.

I felt like asking them if they'd like a go in the

stocks, just to hear them say "No, no" for a change.

"Is it scary?" said Chloe.

Everyone looked at her with their mouths open as up till now she hadn't said a word.

"VERY," said Tumbleweed and all the little witchkins squealed.

We had Hair Styling! after lunch. The teacher, Madam Wiggins, had a skinhead hairdo and dozens of witches hats in different colours. She put on the first one, whipped it off, and had long golden ringlets. Next she had a chestnut pony tail, then a brown bob and on she went for about forty hairdos, all of them disgustrous.

It was clever, but I couldn't help thinking, wasn't there anything more exciting you could do with magic powers than getting a new hairdo? No one else could do any of it except Tumbleweed, who managed a Mohican.

Tumbleweed looked much nicer with the Mohican as it happens, but Wiggins didn't think so.

"Well done, Tumbleweed, but we are trying to make ourselves look *better*, aren't we?" she said.

The rest of the day was more of the same.

Make-up!

"A good witch always looks her good, better, BEST!" said Madam Buggly, who, not to be rude or anything, was no oil painting herself even if her lipstick could change from pink to orange to scarlet every five seconds.

Clothes!

"A witch must always dress for the occasion. Now who wants a spell to change horrible old denims into pretty party dresses?"

All the little witchkins simpered, "Yeth, yeth, yeth."

"And you big girls, would you like lovely ball gowns?"

No, no, no, I thought, although Chloe let me down by whispering, "Mmmmm".

I couldn't help being impressed when Buggly,

who was swathed in a vast emerald green sack, whisked for a second behind her screen and emerged in a dazzling blue number with yellow spots. Next, it was a salmon pink suit with bobbles all over it, then an orange and purple mini skirt and finally a leopard-skin leotard. She had disgustrous dress sense, but it would be quite fun to do that. A puff of smoke later and she was in the sack again.

I thought of poor little Damp, shivering in her single smock, in the stocks.

Voice Class!
"A witch should be able to sing like a bird and growl like a lion," warbled Madam Wheeze. "And she should talk like the Queen of England!"

Deportment!
Madam Ramrod made us walk about with books on our heads for a whole hour. "To straighten your backs!"

And every teacher kept going on with that revolting chant:

"Good better best,
Never let it rest,
Till your good is better
And your better BEST!"

It made me want to scream. But I kept my lip buttoned. I wasn't going to risk showers, or stocks, again.

We flopped on my bed in the evening.

"That was amazing," said Chloe later. "Aren't the teachers brilliant?"

Eh? "If you think learning to talk proper and all that is worth it," I said grumpily. "If I had magic powers I'd use them for something useful."

"Like what?" said Chloe, looking hurt. The trouble with Chloe is she looks hurt too easily.

"Like, like, ice cream for all! No school! Playgrounds on every street!" I felt I wasn't being very convincing. Well, you try it. Think what you would do if you could. It's like having three wishes, you end up wishing for a million pounds and then another million and then all the money in the world. And then you realise you have all the money, like King Midas, but it does you no good because everyone else hasn't got a bean.

"Well, putting an end to wars, then," I said.

"Oh, yes. That would be good," said Chloe.

"Doesn't anyone want to know what Tumbleweed whispered to me about Tabitha?" said Dinah rattily.

I had been dying to know, of course, but all this stupid hairdo and clothes stuff had put sensible things right out of my nut.

"Yes!! What?" I shouted.

"Shhhh," said Dinah. And we went into a huddle. "She said Tabitha has a weak spot."

"Yes? What?"

"She hates music."

"So? Lots of people hate music," I said, pointlessly.

"Yes, but she hates it so much that she has had music banned from Conundrums!"

"Not surprising. They hate fun here," I said, but it suddenly occurred to me that they don't have any music at Hogwarts, either. Maybe witch schools are not all they're cracked up to be. "Anyway, what good does that do us?"

"There is one particular instrument that really scares her."

"So?"

"Trixie, you are clearly not the girl you used to be last week. It must be lack of food," said Dinah in that annoying way people do when they have a Very Extremely good idea going on in their heads but they won't let you in on it.

"Dinah, you are being sarcastic like a teacher."

"Trix! I can't believe you haven't guessed. The instrument Tabitha hates most is the..."

"Trumpet!" I said, the old light bulb of knowledge glowing at last in my brain.

"YES! Now here's the Plan to trap Tabitha Tumultitude..." And she told us her Plan. And it was Very Extremely good.

I'm not going to tell you it now, because it will spoil the suspense. But here's what we needed:

1. Scarlet ink from the Magic Maths room

2. Bonzo

3. Two plastic knives

4. My trumpet

5. My dressing-gown cord

6. Last, but definitely not least, Dinah's brilliant powers of mimicking other people's voices.

"Oooooh, it'll never work," was Chloe's gloomy response.

But I thought it would, and I went to bed feeling almost cheery.

At midnight, me and Dinah and Chloe smuggled a clammy wodge of macaroni cheese and a handful of cold chips out to poor little Damp, shivering in the stocks. I thought it was extremely nice of us to save her some, especially starving yours truly, but she wasn't at all grateful, she just ate it like a starving person, while a huge river of tears flowed down her little white cheeks.

Chapter 6

Next morning at breakfast all the tiny witchkins were squawking away about Tabitha. Tabitha this, Tabitha that, how she could turn old tin mugs into cut glass and a three-legged stool into a four-seater sofa.

How amazingly fascinating. Imagine. You can do anything you like and you choose to turn a three-legged stool into a sofa. (Still I couldn't help thinking at the time that I'd like to learn that spell as well as how to make a matchstick bed into something comfy, which just goes to show

how your ideas can change if you're starving and haven't slept for two days.)

But even Dinah's flattery couldn't get old Tumbleweed to help us with the food spell again.

"I might get expelled!" she whispered. "And I'm going to be going up to the Academy next year."

We ate our gruel while everyone else went "oooh" and "aaaaah," and "You're SO the lucky one".

"Is Damp coming?" asked Dinah innocently.

"Of course not," said Tumbleweed. "She'll be lucky if they let her out before home time."

"Isn't that a teeny bit harsh?" asked Dinah.

"What's the point of having rules if you don't follow them?" asked Tumbleweed. "She deserves the stocks. She's stupid. She was lucky not to get the Bad Girls' Punishment like..."

"Like who?"

"There were three girls last half term, who..."

"Yes?" said Dinah.

Everyone, even the tiniest witchkins, had gone Very Extremely quiet.

Tumbleweed went on: "Who... well, we won't be seeing them again. That's why you're here though, isn't it? So it's a good thing really."

"Yes," smarmed Dinah. "It IS a good thing. I'd never have met YOU, otherwise."

But even this flattery didn't make Tumbleweed look much cheerier. She had gone as white as snow just talking about the Bad Girls.

But pretty soon all the little witchkins were squeaking with joy on the walk to Conundrums Castle, and Tumbleweed was in her element showing Dinah the Stone Giant, the Hanging Tree, the Mad Hermit's Cave and all sorts of other landmarks I'd be really excited about normally, except that all I could think about was the *cup*.

Then we were going past the wishing well! Everyone else dropped pennies in and made a wish, but I kept well clear. Nothing bad happened. Maybe it was safe now? Or was Dad's warning about being *alone* near it?

We went through a little wood, well I hoped it was a little wood and not the forest of doom Dad had warned me about, came into a clearing and gasped.

There was Conundrums itself, towering above us, a mass of stained glass, pointy spires, domes and battlements. It was like every fairytale castle you've ever dreamt of rolled into one. The moat twinkled in the afternoon sunlight and black swans glided about like little boats. When we got closer I realised they *were* little boats. Madam Brute called them by name ("Jocasta",

"Ermintrude" and so on) and they obediently floated up for us to get in, two at a time, and be swanned over the moat.

"No drawbridge," whispered Chloe. "This would be hard to escape from." The same thought was occurring to me. "And only room in the boats for two at a time, so if three of you wanted to leave together, you couldn't."

"Oh shut up, Chloe," I said, watching Dinah giggling in the boat behind with Tumbleweed. I was worried. Dinah wasn't starting to like the disgustrous Tumbleweed, was she?

"Do you think Dinah actually likes Tumbleweed?" said Chloe. If you have a worrying thought you can rely on Chloe to put it into words.

"'Course not," I said, trailing my fingers in the water.

"Aaaaaaaaaaagh!" An enormous tentacle had wrapped itself round my wrist! It was pulling me in! "Help!"

Chloe lurched towards me and grabbed my arm. The boat rocked wildly.

"Samantha! Let go at once," shouted Brute.

"It's not Samantha," I tried to gasp. "It's Chloe, and she's my only hope." But even as I tried to get the words out, the horrible slimy tentacle unwrapped itself and disappeared.

"Samantha is SO naughty," said Brute. "But if I've told you once, I've told you a thousand times.

NEVER put any part of yourself in the Conundrums moat."

Well, it was the first I'd heard of it.

Chloe was shaking like a leaf. Good old Chloe. A friend in need. I hugged her. "You're well strong, Chloe," I said, and she blushed.

But it's a funny old world where girls are called by their surnames and evil monsters of the deep are called Samantha.

Crossing the moat looked as if it would be about a two minute journey, but it took a whole hour to float across because the boats would not go straight. Brute kept chivvying them on, but I think she was really making them zigzag about on purpose.

"It's another way of trapping us," hissed Chloe.

But then we were there. We stepped out on to emerald grass and there was Conundrums, towering above us.

"Amazing," said Chloe, gazing up at the castle as we stepped out. And it was.

We lined up in a crocodile and Brute waved her wand at the moat, which immediately turned into a stormy ocean. "We don't want just anybody to get into Conundrums," she sniffed.

"Or out," whispered Chloe.

"Now, as a special privilege, you may see into the Great Grand Vizier's Hall before we go to the lecture room. You are absolutely forbidden to go elsewhere in the castle or its grounds." Brute mumbled a spell that sounded like open sesame and the great studded wooden door creaked open like in a horror film.

We all gasped. The Great Grand Vizier's Hall was about a mile high. It had stained glass windows at the very top, which threw dancing patterns of coloured light on to the floor below. In the middle was a fountain spouting from the mouth of a gigantic stone dragon.

"That magnificent statue," said Brute, "was made for the great founder of Conundrums himself, the Grand High Vizier, wizard of all the hemispheres."

One of the little witchkins ran giggling towards the fountain and it spurted fire!

"You don't laugh in the presence of the Vizier's dragon," said Brute. "First fire, then the stocks, then..." And everyone shivered. "Now for the Cup and Sorcery lecture," droned Brute, swinging the weeping witchkin over her back like a sack.

The Cup and Sorcery lecture room was like a huge sitting room with a fire blazing in the grate. It was the most welcoming room I'd seen since arriving, although I noticed all the plush chairs had been pushed to the side and a row of wooden benches had been set out for us. The wooden panelled walls were covered in charts of different kinds of tableware. I'd never seen so many kinds of knives and forks in my life. Knives for fish, knives for meat, knives for soup(!), little forks with prongs on (for removing eyes from newts), ladles for broth, other ladles for stew and so on and so on. There were bowls, dishes, platters, saucers, tureens, pans, mugs, cups, tumblers, goblets, chalices, kegs, bottles and jugs in billions of sizes, shapes and colours. It made me tired just looking at them.

We all sat in rows and were given little booklets called: *Cup and Sorcery Techniques for the House Witch*.

"Free of charge," said Brute proudly as if they were the crown jewels. "Now sit quiet as mice." (Why do people say that? We had a mouse in our house once and it scurried about making a terrible din.)

The lights dimmed then flashed like a strobe and Brute announced, "Presenting: the Tremendous, the Terrific, the Titanic, the Tumultuous Tabitha Tumultitude!"

Even my jaw dropped at the sight of Tabitha. She looked about eighteen. She had golden hair all down her back (well, on her head of course, but tumbling all down her back), her eyes were very bright turquoise, like a swimming pool and about twice the length of ordinary normal eyes, and her skin glittered with little flecks of gold and silver to match her dress. If I'd come across her on a beach

I'd have sworn she was a mermaid. And to think dear old Dad turned her down in favour of Mum.

I had horrible butterflies in my stomach at this point, wondering if our Plan had any chance of working, and I had to fight back the urge to shout "thief!", but even with all this going on in my head, I had to admit Tabitha was good. Very good. What my dad would call a "class act".

I don't know if you are interested in cutlery and chinaware. Probably not. A child who is would be a Sad Thing. But you know how it is that some teachers can make Very Extremely interesting things, like say, kings having their heads cut off, into Very Extremely boring things? Well, I hate to admit it, but Tabitha was the opposite. Even with something so disgustrously boring as washing-up, or laying the table, she made it seem like your wildest dream come true.

She warmed up with a bit of plate spinning like the Chinese circus, then she transformed various old chipped mugs with Simpsons on like the ones we have at home into the kind of thing the Queen wouldn't turn her nose up at. Then she made a whole row of plastic beakers into a flowery tea service with a pot full of tea, milk jug, sugar bowls and all. Then she got all the cups to line up like in *Beauty and the Beast* and the teapot bounced about on its own, filling them while the cups squawked "two sugars", or "just lemon" and all the teeniest witchkins became hysterical with excitement.

The last bit was like *Fantasia* with all the dishes washing themselves. I was mesmerised. It was like watching fireworks. Chloe was staring at Tabitha in adoration like everyone else and I had to kick her on the ankle and pinch myself hard to break the spell.

Then Tabitha turned to us, bowed very low and spoke in a voice that sounded like fairy bells tinkling. Which was odd, for someone who hated music. "Some of you bigger ones *will* be coming to Conundrums next year, and although I won't have the pleasure—" here, she sneered "—of teaching you until Year Thirteen, I shall be delighted to answer any questions you may have."

My stomach turned over. Would our Plan work? I was afraid Dinah might have been put under Tabitha's spell and would forget what to do. All the little witchkins were waving their hands madly hoping to be picked.

But just as I was about to give up, an eerie Voice echoed round the room:

"*I have a question, an urgent question,*
One that may give you indigestion."

A couple of witchkins giggled, but Tabitha only looked slightly startled for a moment, smoothed her dress and said, "Wait your turn whoever that is." And she pointed to a minute witchkin in the front row. "What would YOU like to ask?" But before the witchkin could reply, the Voice came again, louder:

"*I have a question, own up own up,*
Where, oh where, is my precious cup?"

Tabitha smirked. "There are thousands of cups."

"No!" shrieked the Voice. "Where is MY cup?"

Tabitha looked uncomfortable. "Which cup?"

"*I think you know, I think you know –*
The cup you stole so long ago," squealed the Voice.

"HOW DARE YOU!" hissed Tabitha, her voice sounding nothing like fairy bells after all, but more like a nest of vipers. Brute and Wiggins were scurrying around trying to find the culprit. But everyone knew this wasn't a child's voice. It sounded like, well, like a ghost.

Tabitha turned to leave the hall, her eyes

flaming with fury. The pupils had literally turned red. It was scary. Now I could see why Dad preferred Mum.

"What nonsense!" she stormed. "I won't waste my time on these stupid apprentices again!"

"We're not stupid," muttered a couple of witchkins, thoroughly put out. It was the first sign of spirit from any of them and I felt like cheering.

The Voice continued:

"Give it up, give it up,

My demons will retrieve this *cup*."

And then there was a strange noise like an elephant blowing its nose. FAAAAAAAARN, MNWHAWWWWW. I should have given Dinah lessons, for of course you have guessed she was being the Voice. But I also knew she was blowing my trumpet at that point, and Tabitha knew it was a trumpet too, even if nobody else did. She froze.

I nudged Chloe. Time for Stage Two of our Plan. Chloe had a chance to show she really can be a good drama queen if she wants. She fell to the ground fighting an invisible thing and screaming at the top of her little voice. "No!" she shouted. "It isn't me! It isn't me! I don't know what cup you mean!"

Everyone rushed to see what was attacking Chloe and then it was my turn. I screamed, fell flat on my face (it was a Very Extremely impressive fall, not to boast) and started kicking and struggling as though some heavy thing was on top of me. "No! No!" I cried. "I've never seen the stupid *cup*!"

The Ghostly Voice echoed again, much much louder:

"No, not those innocent babies!
Go for Tabitha! Give her rabies!
She is the one who stole the *cup*!
Forthwith, send in the Demon Pup!"

And then the best bit happened. Bonzo (brilliantly disguised as a little black dog by yours truly, by rolling him in coal dust just like in *101 Dalmations*) leapt at Tabitha, with a note in his mouth. It worked. He did look quite scary actually, because we had made some very realistic plastic horns out of a couple of plastic knives from the kitchen and we'd lengthened his tail with my dressing gown cord, which we'd stuck a black cardboard arrow head on the end of, so he looked exactly like a tiny devil.

Tabitha was obviously convinced he was an evil spirit. She tore the note from his mouth and fled.

Next thing, me and Chloe were the centre of attention, everyone was shouting "What happened? Are you all right?" and all, whatever. We said we had been overwhelmed by invisible spirits who told us they were from an evil witch.

"There's no such thing as witches," said Brute. "I mean, evil witches and invisible spirits, of course." She looked a bit flustered as all the little witchkins were staring at her like a treacherous traitor. Well, it's a bit of a silly thing to say if you're running a witches' school.

"Well, what was it then?" said Tumbleweed, who had stopped looking snooty and was just looking scared.

"Hysteria, I expect," said Brute. "It's too hot in here."

"No, what was the Voice?" said Dinah.

Of course, Dinah had been the Voice, but she had smuggled herself back into the room and no one knew except me and Chloe.

"Oh, I think it was a trick of Tabitha's," said Brute uncertainly. "She loves to scare the witchkins, to see if they are tough enough for Conundrums."

"But she looked scared herself," piped up a tiny witchkin, too small to know better.

"Nonsense!" thundered Brute. "Nothing scares Tabitha Tumultitude!"

"But that Voice," continued Dinah. "That Voice was saying that Tabitha stole a cup. What would be the point of that?"

"I have never heard anything so ridiculous in my life!" stormed Brute. "Tabitha Tumultitude a thief! Absurd! There was absolutely nothing about a cup. Except of course her magnificent display of the mysteries of Cup and Sorcery."

"Absolutely," piped up Madam Wiggins. "There was something about a pup, I think. Tabitha loves animals, of course, such a kind person..."

"She didn't seem to like that Demon Pup," said Dinah.

"Nonsense! No such thing!" said Brute. "Unless you mean that piece of hot coal that must have rolled out of the grate. You have the kind of imagination," she added, "that may need cooling in a cold shower."

What? Was she really trying to pretend that Bonzo was a piece of COAL? I had scooped him up into my bag and was hugging him through it to keep him quiet. I couldn't wait to get out of there before he gave the game away.

"But it did say stealing a cup..." whispered the brave midget witchkin, shortly before bursting into tears at the sight of Brute, who silenced her with the stare of a Gorgon. Not for the first time, I thought longingly of old Warty-Beak.

"Young witches," bellowed Brute, "should be seen and not heard. Now I want absolute silence for the rest of the trip! You are all to spend this evening composing thank you letters to Tabitha for her splendid demonstration."

And so we all trailed out and into the swan boats in silence. But I could see everyone was thinking hard. They knew Brute was lying. Good. Stages One and Two of our Master Plan had gone brilliantly. But would Stage Three of the Plan work? The butterflies in my tummy seemed to have turned into bats and the ride across the moat was choppy, which made me feel even sicker. Brute was punishing us by making it stormy, what a cheek. On top of that, Bonzo was squeaking and wriggling like a loony in my rucksack. I had to pretend to have the most disgustrous sneezing attack in order to cover up his noise. Hey, animal lovers, this wasn't cruel, I'd put about six tons of food and all his favourite toys in with him.

Oh, I guess I'd better tell you now what was in the note that Bonzo gave to Tabitha, so you can get nervous too. Here it is:

The spirits of seventeen generations of Tempests are gathered together this week to retrieve the *cup* you stole from Tobias Tempest.

If you return this *cup* by midnight tonight, all will be well.

You are to leave it by the well next to the apprentices' hut.

If you leave it by the well, all will be well.

If not, you'll be engulfed by the Gorgonzola spell!

P.S. Tabitha Tumultitude, since you know NOTHING compared to seventeen generations of Tempests, you may not have heard of the Gorgonzola spell.

It turns you, not into stone, but into CHEESE. You will still be able to move about but you are certain to be rejected by all your friends and are likely to end your life quite soon as a result of being eaten by mice.

Most of this was written by Chloe, who is good at that sort of thing, but I made the Gorgonzola spell up, of course, rather good, not to boast or anything. But would it work? Would we get the *cup* at midnight? I tumbled into a half sleep, filled with nightmares of wicked mermaids and stormy moats...

Chapter 7

At ten minutes to midnight, I sat up in horror. Chloe had asked Tabitha to put the *cup* by the well. And Dad had told me not to go near the well. So much had been happening that I hadn't had time to tell Dinah and Chloe about these warnings... How could I have been so stupid? Well, I couldn't let them know now, they would kill me.

They tapped on my door a few seconds later, so I didn't have any more time to worry about it.

I grabbed my dressing gown and we crept outside and made our way to the little clearing where the well stood. Perhaps it isn't the wishing well, I thought to myself. Perhaps it's just any old well. But I knew perfectly well it was the wishing well because the only light, which seemed to be a lantern made of glow-worms, was flickering above a big sign saying:

WELCOME TO YE WISHINGE WELLE
WHERE WISHES WILL COME TRUE
UNLESS YOU DARE TO BREAK THE SPELLE
WHICH SPELLS THE ENDE FOR YOU.

"I don't like the look of it," whispered Chloe.

"If you were looking at Disneyland covered in marshmallows would you like the look of that?" snapped Dinah.

But it wasn't just Chloe who was feeling creepy. The whole glade was rustling in a creepy way and I had a horrible feeling we were being watched by something Not at All Nice. We strained our eyes to see through the inky darkness.

"She hasn't done it, let's go," said Chloe.

"No, wait!" said Dinah. "Look!"

I peered ahead and saw a faint gleam. I peered harder. It *was* the *cup*. And Tabitha had left it right beside the well. Oh lordy. "Don't go near the well." Dad's words were pounding in my head.

"Right, let's get it," said Dinah.

"Yes, you go," I said, feeling relieved. I mean, Dad only said it to me, didn't he? It was probably fine for anyone else to go. Then, "NO," I hissed. "We should wait half an hour, in case Tabitha's lurking about to lay a trap."

"But it's freezing," whispered Chloe.

Then I told them what Dad had said about the well.

"You moron," said Dinah to Chloe. "Why'd you tell Tabitha to go to the well? You could have said anywhere."

I could see this wasn't fair. After all, I had completely forgotten to tell them about Dad's warning in his letter. It would have to be me who went to get the *cup*. I couldn't send my friends to certain doom.

"It's not her fault, it's mine," I said. "I'll get it and you two stay here."

"NO," said Dinah. "We need a long pole."

"Pole?" I said in a stupid sort of way.

"Pole," she said. "With a hook on, so we can hook it."

"Or a magnet," said Chloe.

"Oh SURE. There's bound to be a magnet lying about," said Dinah sarcastically.

"Wait," I said. "Lasso!"

"But where are we going to find a lasso?" said Chloe.

"Dressing gowns," I said. So we tied our dressing gown cords together. And my Very Extremely long one made it possible to make a quite good lasso.

"Thank you, Mum," I whispered to myself.

We threw the lasso about fifty times and then, plonk, it went round the *cup* and we tugged it gently towards us.

YES! Success! It was beautiful. It was golden. It glowed all by itself.

BLeeeEEEEARK BLEeeeeARK

"What was that?"

We had no time to wonder – a foul tentacle, like Samantha's, had curled up out of the well and whisked the *cup* out of my hands like a lasso.

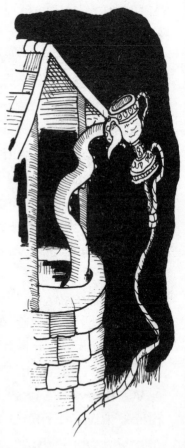

"No! It's going to drop it in the well!"

And then, I swear, I heard a voice I knew, but I couldn't place it. "Go Flossie GO! FETCH!" it shouted. And a huge animal, that seemed half dog, half dragon, with eyes like yellow saucers and fangs like sabres, came

146

bounding out of the wood howling like a herd of banshees. It leapt at the tentacle, bit it clean in half, picked up the *cup* in its fangs and hurtled straight towards us. We all screamed but all it did was drop the *cup* in my lap and race off.

"Good girl, Flossie. See you later, Trixie. Run for your life, there's more in the well," came the strangely familiar voice. And as it spoke, a dozen more tentacles came snaking out of the well, writhing towards us.

So we ran for our lives, and we could hear the slithering of the tentacles, and the squelching of their disgustrous suckers, but they couldn't quite catch us.

We tore back to the school, raced up to my room and wedged the stool against the door, but even those tentacles were not long enough to follow us all that way. We fell on the bed panting.

"Who was that who saved us in the wood?" gasped Chloe. "Whoever it was knew your name."

"I know. But I don't know," I said, gazing awestruck at the *cup*.

We all gazed.
It was golden.
It was beautiful.
It shimmered
like a magical thing,
which of course it was.
And the writing on it sparkled and shimmered.

"Like diamonds," sighed Chloe.

"They are diamonds," I said proudly, and then panicked. Dad had said to check his name was on it, but I hadn't had a chance, what with lassos and tentacles and now all I could make out were the words "Conundrums Cup" but nothing else.

Then I remembered, Dad had told me you had to breathe on it for the names to appear. I sighed on it like you do on a window to write a message, and a long list of moving, sparkling names appeared. It went on and on, rolling up the *cup*

like film credits, through the alphabet until the Ts. And there was Dad's name, at the end of a long list of Tempests: Tobias Terrapin Turtle Tempest. In diamonds!

"Turtle?" said Dinah.

"Terrapin?" said Chloe.

Curses.

"If you tell anyone at school about this I will never speak to you ever again," I said.

It was 2 a.m. I was Very Extremely knackered.

"Put it under your mattress," hissed Dinah.

"Home tomorrow," sighed Chloe.

YES. Home tomorrow. With the *cup*. I couldn't wait.

I shoved the *cup* under the mattress and fell on top of it, dressing gown and all. And even though that pebble mattress was even lumpier with a huge *cup* under it, it felt like it was made of fairy wings and candy floss and I fell into the deepest sleep I've ever fallen into. But not for long.

NEE NAW NEE NAW

I thought I was dreaming about Tomato playing police. But I wasn't. They were real police sirens.

And they were in my room! (Not the sirens, the police.)

There were two enormous police officers standing by my bed.

"Out you get," said one, who was the smaller of the two, not more than six feet tall and no wider than a shed. "Now let's look under here," she said, whisking the pebble mattress off and revealing the *cup*. You may wonder why I didn't hide it in a better place. But where else was there to hide it?

"My *cup*! My lovely, lovely *cup*!" squealed a disgustrously familiar voice. And there was Tabitha, shimmering in the doorway.

"You've got a lot of explaining to do young lady," said the police officer, and she grabbed me by my ear as I tried to run between her legs.

Tabitha cackled a high witchy cackle like a chain saw and clutched the *cup*.

"Gerroff! Leave me alone!" I shouted, trying to

bite the police officer. "It's my dad's! It's got his name on it."

Police Sergeant Bungle, as I later discovered she was called, squinted at the *cup*.

"It's magic," I squeaked. "You have to breathe on it to read it."

"Oh yes," said Sergeant Bungle. "Oh yes. And the moon is made of cheese." But she was panting with the effort of holding me and the writing started to appear! Her eyes were Very Extremely poppy to begin with, but now they were like footballs.

"See?" I said.

"Hmmm, funny name for a bloke," said Bungle. And she showed me the *cup*. It had one name on it: Tabitha Tumultitude.

"Is your dad's name Tabitha?" she said, not very nicely.

The even bigger officer, Constable Yogi, whipped out a notebook. "Anything you say will be taken down and may be used in evidence," he barked. I would have said, "pants" but I was not in the mood.

By now the whole school was awake and twenty

squawking witchkins were trying to cram into my room. I signed frantically to Chloe and Dinah not to say anything, but of course they did.

"She didn't steal it. It's hers."

"If she's guilty then we are too. We were with her."

But the police didn't seem that interested. "The stolen property was in her room. We can't arrest dozens of girls at once. We'll deal with you lot later," they said.

"I can't let a Conundrums apprentice be taken on her own, however much standards may have dropped in this establishment," Mope muttered under her breath, as Brute shot her a furious look.

So then Mope and I were whisked into the police van and driven away.

"You will be allowed one telephone call at the station," said Bungle.

I was desperate to ring Mum, but in the van, I had a brainwave and when we got to the station I said, "I want to ring my grandmother, Eugenia Eudora Anaconda Tempest, High Priestess of Egg."

All the police put their fingers on their

foreheads and rolled their eyes as if I was a loony, which was fine by me.

But when I phoned Grandma Tempest, she was furious. "Do you know what TIME it is? Trixie WHO?" she said. I keep forgetting she has hundreds of relatives.

"Granddaughter number thirty," I said. "You paid for me to go to Conundrums." Then I tried to tell her the story but she wasn't listening.

"Arrested! Fool!" she fumed. "I suppose I'll have to fly over and get you. What a frightful BORE."

Two seconds later, I kid-you-not, there was a flash, a puff of smoke and there she was. Even Bungle looked impressed.

Grandma Tempest is a rather unusual person, even by witchy standards. She is seven feet tall, for a start, which dwarfed Bungle and Yogi. And she has her hair done purple and piled right on top like Marge in *The Simpsons*, which makes her about as high as most ceilings. She was wearing a purple lycra jump suit.

"Forgive the informal attire, Officer," she said charmingly, "I was doing my exercise video. Now what's this little ruffian been up to?"

53

If she was doing her exercise video at three in the morning, then why was she so cross about the time? I thought. But I managed to get my version of the story in, and Grandma T calmed down.

"Aaaaaah," she said. "Tabitha. Hmmmmm." And the way she said it meant she knew that Tabitha spelt Trouble.

The police showed Grandma T the *cup*.

"See?" said Bungle. "It's obviously not your granddaughter's."

"But then why would Tabitha have left it by the well?" I said. "And why would she have told the police to search MY room? She must have known it was me who wrote the note, because it WAS my dad's *cup*. She must have looked up the names of all the apprentices and seen 'Tempest'."

"Of course," said Grandma T.

"Nonsense," tinkled a disgustrous voice. It was Tabitha, who had followed us to the police station. She was wearing a scarlet leotard with scarlet tights and her talons were painted gold. "SO sorry you've been put to all this trouble, Officer," she said to Yogi with a dazzling smile. "I was spying on the well. That's how I knew it was this little cockroach who stole MY *cup*. Naturally I wanted to catch the revolting kids who tried to ruin my presentation to the apprentices. I'm sure YOU understand that, Officer; a woman alone has to protect herself. So I used my own *cup* as a lure for them. I have now come to reclaim MY property."

"Certainly, madam," said Yogi, who had turned a luminous pink. "And may I say that is a most beautiful, er, dress." He was staring at Tabitha like Bonzo staring at a Fidoburger. He took the *cup* off Bungle and drifted towards Tabitha in a trance.

"Tabitha!" cried Grandma T. "How lovely to see you. It's been so long."

As Grandma Tempest turned round, Tabitha took a step backwards in alarm. She obviously thought I was just with Mope, who was wheezing dejectedly in the corner muttering about how things were better in the Good Old Days.

"Eugenia!" tinkled Tabitha. "I didn't know you were still alive!"

"But darling," whispered Grandma T, "I'm only 300. And JUST as lively as when you were dating Tobias. Don't you remember?"

"I don't know what you're talking about. All I want is my *cup*, which has been stolen, by this, this insect!"

Grandma T remained Very Extremely calm. "I'm sure there's been a little mix-up but you must remember that there is a simply splendid old spell for identifying lost property. I think now would be a very good time to use it."

Tabitha turned a sickly shade of green. "Nonsense! I've never seen this woman before in my life, Officer. She obviously thinks she is a witch. Mad as a hatter."

"WHAT?" I gasped. "But YOU'RE a witch yourself."

"I most certainly am NOT," snarled Tabitha. "I don't believe in such nonsense. I just put on shows for stupid kids. Now, I have better things to do," and Tabitha grabbed the _cup_ and turned to go.

"A witch! How dare you?" said Grandma T.

At that point I realised they were both trying to keep it secret from the police that they were real witches.

"I just want one more look, please, Officer, at the _cup_," said Grandma T. "After all, it is my granddaughter's honour that's at stake."

Bungle and Yogi looked confused. But Grandma had swiftly shot out her foot and tripped Tabitha, who fell flat on her face. The _cup_ flew neatly into Grandma T's hand.

Then Grandma T whispered something and breathed on the _cup_. Tabitha's name on the _cup_ quivered, turned blue and flew off screaming. A whole row of new names appeared. And there was Dad's!

"It's marvellous, isn't it? What you can get at

joke shops these days?" she said to Bungle. "I think it must have been a trick of the light that made Tobias Tempest look like Tabitha Tumultitude, don't you? And your middle names are Turtle and Terrapin too, aren't they, Tabitha? Such lovely names. That's why I chose them for dear Tobias."

Tabitha was defeated. She changed colour a few times and I could see she wanted to spin her head round and spit fire, but she didn't dare do it in a police station.

"You're coming with me," she snarled, grabbing poor old Mope. "If you want to keep your JOB." And she swept out, pulling poor little Mope along with her.

"Well, that's all settled then, ladies," said Bungle, who was very relieved, I think, to see them go.

Yogi dashed out into the rain after Tabitha and put his jacket down in the mud for her to walk over.

squelch
squelch

"So you won't get those enchanting shoes wet."

"Thank you, scum," she said, leaping into her emerald-green sports car and zooming off, splattering mud all over Yogi. The last I saw of him he was just standing there looking after her with a stupid smile on his mug.

Grandma Tempest drove me back in an old banger that must have been made before the war.

"Why don't you ride a broom?" I asked.

"Because it is extremely important for witches to seem like ordinary people," she said. "Otherwise we would all be hunted down and drowned or burnt, like in the Bad Old Days. Anyway, this car flies when I need it to."

"But you could just turn people into stone and stuff."

"I could, but I wouldn't. No good witch would ever do such a thing."

"But the witches at Conundrums are horrible," I said.

"Are they?" she said, but I didn't think she was listening.

"It's horrendous and disgustrous," I said. "They

put people in the stocks!"

"Oh come on now. I think you're being over-imaginative," she said.

"They do, they do!"

"Listen, Conundrums may not be what it was in MY day, but no witches' academy would ever descend to such behaviour," she said sternly. "Please don't let me hear you lying again."

Adults never listen. I thought witches might be different, but it seems they are worse. I changed the subject. "Will Tabitha get the sack?" I asked.

"Of course. That means she will have to wear a sack and clean the Conundrums loos with a toothbrush."

"Heh heh! How long for?"

"Ooh, twenty years, I should think."

Just as we were about to turn into the road for the half-term taster hut, Grandma T stopped the car.

"Now, Tamsin, there's something I wanted to ask you."

"Trixie."

"Tamsin, Trixie, it doesn't matter. What I want to know is why you were so keen to retrieve Tobias's cup."

I told her about the money.

"Money? You can't SELL a Conundrums *cup*!" That *cup* has been won by generations of Tempests. It's the Snarg *cup*! It's priceless."

"That's why we want to sell it."

"Well, I forbid it," she sighed. "How much money does your father want?"

I whispered the huge amount of money that Dad owes. I whispered that we were going to be thrown out of our house unless we paid it.

"I TOLD him not to marry a teacher," she huffed. "I always said: marry for money, not love. Never mind, it's peanuts." And then she took out a cheque book and wrote me a cheque to give to Dad.

"But that's two hundred pounds more than we need," I said.

"One hundred pounds for you and one for your little sister, or is it a brother?" she muttered.

"Oh thank you, thank you, thank you!" I shouted. "Lovely Grandma Tempest!" and I flung

my arms round her and kissed her. She blushed.

"Goodness, you have certainly got a lot of teacher blood in you, witches NEVER hug," she said. But I could tell she liked it. "Tell Tobias I'm not made of money and he can't have any more unless he comes to see me himself," she said. And she looked a little bit sad. "Goodbye dear, I'm not coming into the school with you. I'm not very popular there at present," she said.

"You do know it's horrible then. Why did you send me?" I asked.

"It sounds as though things are getting worse than I thought," she said. "I'll look into it, when I have the time." And she drove off, looking almost like an ordinary old lady in her little old car.

I turned into the drive clutching my cheque and the *cup* and saw all the little witchkins with their bags all packed, waiting for the talking horses to take them to the train.

Chapter 8

They all cheered when they saw me, even Mope. Dinah and Chloe and Bonzo and the pekes and me did a little war dance with the *cup*, and Tumbleweed gave me an envelope.

"Read it later," she whispered. Lordy, was

Tumbleweed trying to make up? I stuffed it into my dressing-gown pocket, as Mope tapped me on the shoulder.

"It's more than my job's worth to say this, Tempest, but you ought to tell the world what's going on here," she hissed.

"Don't worry, I will," I said. "Where's Damp?"

"Ooh lawks, we forgot all about her," said Mope.

We raced off to the stocks to free Damp. We had to batter at the wood till it burst open because Brute had lost the keys, and poor little Damp fell out weeping.

"I want to see Bart," was all she could say at first.

"Bart?" I said, remembering the voice in the woods and the boy I met on the coach and putting two and two together. "Does he have ginger hair?"

It turned out that Daisy Damp was Bart's sister! He had run away from Conundrums Academy and she had tried to help him. That was why she was in the stocks.

"But *HE* helped *US*," I said and told her about the creature by the well.

"Oh that sounds like Flossie, all right," said Daisy, smiling for the first time for a week. "Listen, you've got to save me. I'm supposed to be going to Conundrums next term and if I do I will die," she whispered. "You've got to help me get Bart out, too. And rescue the Bad Girls and... and..."

"What was that, Damp?" Brute loomed over us.

Almost immediately, we were all bundled into coaches. I couldn't see Merlin, or Daisy, or Mope. But I knew I would have to come back...

On the way home, me and Dinah and Chloe read Tumbleweed's note:

Tempest,

If you come near Conundrums again the Evil Force will mince you.

"That's weedy," snorted Dinah.

"I think she means it. She wrote it like that on purpose so that if Trixie shows it to an adult they'll just dismiss it as a silly schoolgirl prank," said Chloe.

"Hmm, clever," said Dinah. "Let's see what she wrote to me."

Dear Dinah,

(I hope you don't mind me using your first name.) I am going to get my parents to get you a place at Conundrums next year.

YOU are just the kind of girl we need. See you then!

Best wishes

Tumbleweed

"Wow. You certainly fooled her," I said.

"Why didn't she write to me?" said Chloe. "Obviously she doesn't think I count."

"Oh Chloe, she's FOUL," we both said. "You don't need her, you've got us."

So that was how I got to go to witches' school.

I don't need to tell you how Very Extremely delighted Mum and Dad and Tomato were when I got back with the cheque and the *cup*, even though Mum made a great big thing of not wanting to take the money off Grandma Tempest

and I had to really struggle not to tell her everything, first because I promised Dad, but second because I knew they'd never let me go back if they knew how foul Conundrums was. And I had a feeling I was going to have to get back, somehow...

* * *

But me and Dinah and Chloe have got an awful lot of Big Questions. First, how can we tell anyone about our adventure? No one except Dad would believe a word of it, because no magic works outside Conundrums until you are eighteen and have taken your big exams. But second, was Conundrums really a witchy school at all?

"That talking loo could have been a tape recording," said Dinah.

"And the talking horses?" I asked sadly.

"The magic food could have just been brought in while we had our eyes closed," said Chloe. "Remember how we asked for nut roast, but we got macaroni cheese instead?"

"The hairdos could have just been stuffed inside Madam Wiggins' hat," I added.

"I think maybe they are all just really good conjurors, from the Magic Circle, or somewhere, and they are using the school to get money from rich parents who want their kids to be magic," said Dinah.

"Whatever they are, they're foul and dangerous, though," said Chloe gloomily.

"But Grandma Tempest IS a real witch. I know she is," I said. "And my dad says so too. Anyway, look how magic the *cup* is."

"Hmmm. Maybe," said Dinah. "But perhaps real

witches are dying out and the people running Conundrums want to keep it going to make money."

"Maybe the school has been taken over by a few Bad Witches, like Tabitha, and a lot of conjurors. Anyway, it's like a prison. And it should be stopped," said Chloe.

"But still, we don't know for sure, maybe the real Academy is nothing like the half-term taster course," said Dinah. Obviously Tumbleweed's promise to get her a place was turning her head.

"But what about Daisy Damp?" I cried, shocked.

"You never know, maybe she did something really bad..." murmured Dinah dreamily.

"And deserved the stocks?!" I was outraged.

"Look, whatever's going on, we are going to find out, aren't we?" said Dinah, winking at me.

"It's a deal," I said.

And then we all solemnly swore not to tell anyone anything until we had worked out a Plan...

And as I fell into my lovely comfy bed with my lovely Harpo and Bonzo and all the other puppies,

I thought to myself, I will go back. I want to find out the secret of Conundrums. I will go back and help out Daisy and Bart and the Bad Girls and Mope and Merlin.

On second thoughts, maybe not...
The Evil Force might mince me.

and The Amazing
Talking Dog

by Ros Asquith

Trixie has more on her mind than boy bands and butterfly
tattoos, she's out to Save the World. But first she needs
cash, and fast, before Mum and Dad find out she's lost
her precious trumpet. Enter Harpo, her amazing, talking,
singing, yap-artist dog. Is this hound-with-a-sound
too good to be true? Read and believe!

HarperCollins *Children's Books*

Trixie Tempest

and the Ghost of
St Aubergine's

by Ros Asquith

Someone is playing ghostly tricks on the staff and pupils of
St Aubergine's School. But it isn't Trixie Tempest, oh no!
She is far too busy Saving the Planet, being Nice to Nits and
practising her solo for the Save the World with a Song
Concert. So just who can it be? Not a real ghost, surely?

Oh No-o-o-o-o-o-o-o-o-o-o-o-o-o-o-o-o-o-o-o

A second adventure for the tweenage tearaway with a heart
of gold and a brain full of fireworks.

HarperCollins *Children's Books*

Trixie Tempest's

ABZ of Life

by Ros Asquith

Trixie Tempest is every tweenage girl's best friend. She's even
written a Very Extremely handy book full of tweenage tips.
So if you've got a question, look up the answer in Trixie's ABZ of life.
She can give you advice on topics such as:

Dogs (how to choose one to suit you)

Jellyfish (isn't nature wonderful?)

Rude Noises (with a Very Extremely funny farting poem)

And it's all in alphabetical order too, so it's really easy to look
stuff up. Remember - worries go away when Trixie has her say!

HarperCollins *Children's Books*